SUZANNE & GERTRUDE

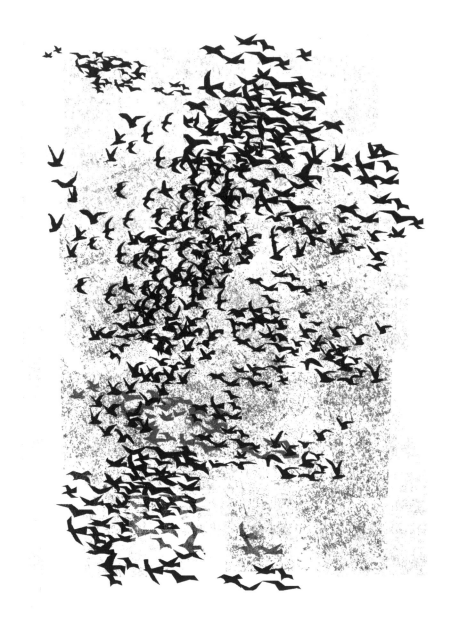

SUZANNE AND GERTRUDE

A NOVEL BY JEB LOY NICHOLS

PUSHCART PRESS
WAINSCOTT, NEW YORK

Illustrations by Jeb Loy Nichols
Designed by Mary Kornblum

ISBN 978-1-888889-98-7

Published by Pushcart Press
P.O. Box 380   Wainscott, NY 11975

Distributed by WW Norton & Company, Inc
500 Fifth Avenue   New York, NY 10110

FIRST EDITION

This book is for my sister and for Mary
And as always for Loraine

There is too much talk about loving.
Most of us are strangers to ourselves
but we are strangers together and in
that way it is possible to live.
• PETER S. FEIBLEMAN

We do not comprehend ruins until we
are ourselves in ruin.
• HEINRICH HEINE

The surface is forever a hoax,
a commonplace, uninteresting thing
for kids to waste time on.
• DOROTHY BAKER

Ask the owl about the darkness.
• KEVIN McILVOY

FEBRUARY

The donkey wasn't there and then suddenly, amongst the whited weeds, it was. She doesn't see it arrive. It had come silently, using its own system of navigation; she wonders tentatively about fences and streams and public footways and gates and cattle grids. How has it managed to migrate from where it was to where it is? How has it found her? Why is it standing there that way, staring? She turns to the dim room; tomorrow it'll be gone. These things happen out here, in the hills, in the winter. Animals, weeds, trees, cars, neighbours, husbands, weather; things appear and then, without warning, vanish.

The sky, swimming with heavy clouds, is neither grey nor white nor dark nor clear.

Earlier she had stayed in bed an extra hour where it was warm and private, beneath a duvet and two blankets. In nothing but a t-shirt. Getting up meant pulling on layer upon layer of clothing, filling the wood basket, starting a fire in the stove, wiping the frost and condensation from the windows. It meant toast and coffee and an egg. Getting up meant another day.

Now she sits in her chair, sips her tea and stares at the donkey. They share a similar blankness; large motionless eyes, heavily lashed and lidded. The donkey appears to be all over ashen grey, moving only enough to feed itself, bending to the cold grass, chewing, and straightening. There's a tuft of white near its nose. Its tail flickers.

She puts more wood in the stove and wraps a shawl around her shoulders. Finally, after an hour, the donkey takes seven steps to its left. Suzanne, sitting in near darkness, asks, is that it? That all you got?

She goes into the kitchen, takes a bag of soup from the freezer, transfers it to a pot, turns on the electric cooker, and returns to her chair. The donkey hasn't moved.

A crow floats above the fields. The cold closes the world. Distances are rearranged, time is foreshortened. It reduces movement, lulls the mind. She watches a fox cut quickly across the field, moving towards the stream in the way foxes do, as if floating. Betwixt the alders and hawthorns. There's a sound here that has to do with breeze rushing down from the hills, the collision of dead leaves and wind, that can wound her. Cut her open and leave her for dead.

On most days she leaves the house at 8:00, opens the shop at 9:00, leaves it at 5:00, and is home by 5:30. The shop, ten miles away, is closed Saturday afternoon, and all day Sunday and

Monday. The front door is a pale greyish green. Above the door, in gold script, it says, The Sewing Basket. A bell rattles when people enter. Suzanne's lunch, brought from home, is pasta in a plastic tub. She alternates sauces – pesto, marinara, alfredo, carbonara. People know her. She has brown hair that, seen in certain lights, appears red. A sign near the counter, unchanged for five years, says: All Fabric Sold by the Meter / Off Cuts Available / Buttons and Cotton Individually Marked / Zippers, Clasps and Hooks Under Counter. Another sign, by the door, says: Be Better To Your Neighbours and You'll Have Better Neighbours. Another sign, over the bolts of fabrics, says: Buy Local.

Suzanne takes home two hundred pounds a week. The shop is small and moderately busy.

In the morning she calls Dorothy.

Dorothy, she says, I'm looking at a donkey.

A donkey?

Standing right there. In my field.

A donkey?

A flesh and blood donkey.

Whose is it?

No idea.

Where'd it come from?

No idea.

Dorothy keeps ducks, two horses, a pony, a dog, several cats, five chickens and a dozen sheep.

A husband too, named Morris. She has an old Land Rover, a tractor, and an enormous garden.

Is it, asks Dorothy, a he or a she?

No idea.

Does it have an ear tag?

Can't see one.

Is it approachable? Is it tame?

Don't know.

Must have wandered down along the stream, says Dorothy.

Suzanne nods.

I can make some calls, says Dorothy. I spoze. See if anyone's missing a donkey.

Thanks.

Does it look hungry?

What the hell does a hungry donkey look like?

Thin, says Dorothy.

A cold rain. The days are getting shorter. Smaller birds and rodents disappear into holes and nooks, as far from humans as possible, to spend the night and the winter in peace.

Suzanne and Dorothy stand amidst wilted cow parsley and burdock, iced puddles and brittled branches. The donkey blows out air noisily. Dorothy gives it a friendly pat on the neck. Suzanne tentatively strokes it's flank.

It's a she, says Dorothy. That's good sign.

Is it?

Almost always.

And she's used to people, says Dorothy. Another good sign.

Suzanne isn't at all sure that being used to people is a good sign. She gently touches the stiff hair at the base of its mane.

And no spring chicken. Says Dorothy. I'd say fifteen years old.

Suzanne nods, and asks, what do I do?

I've no idea.

She must belong to someone.

Must she?

Yes. Says Suzanne. She must.

Dorothy crouches and examines the donkey's hooves.

Everything belongs to someone. Says Suzanne.

Dorothy looks up over her shoulder and says, do you?

Suzanne doesn't answer.

They have chocolate biscuits and milky tea. It's three-thirty and already dusk. Suzanne wears a green knit jumper. The chocolate biscuits are not home made. There's no sunlight anywhere, just shadows. The day is flat. They each wear slippers. No point, Dorothy says, calling the animal welfare officer.

The who?

Only tell you there's nothing they can do unless

you can identify the owner. So long as it's healthy and upright they don't want to know.

Suzanne nods. She puts down her tea and stands. Goes over and flips on the light. The light doesn't quite fill the room.

Looks to me, says Dorothy, until you hear otherwise, you got yourself a donkey.

Do I?

Suzanne's slippers are red felt. Dorothy's were once Hillman's, brown corduroy, gone over at the back.

Till someone comes round and claims it.

Suzanne finishes her biscuit.

Someone. She says.

First things first, says Dorothy.

Suzanne pushes back and does something with her arms.

I'll bring you over some hay. Says Dorothy.

Hay?

Coupla bales.

They each turn towards the window. The donkey is barely visible. Everything out there is grey. Their own reflections stare back at them. Dorothy's face hovers in a dark circle of hair.

Suzanne nods and says, thanks.

In the morning Suzanne spreads out a handful of hay. She's been doing this for an hour, pulling at hay and dropping it at the donkey's hooves. The donkey bends and lips the hay. Suzanne watches its jaws work. She listens to it chew. The whole furred length of it quivers. After a minute it swivels and thrusts its nose at Suzanne.

What?

The donkey pushes its nose at Suzanne's hands.

More?

Suzanne turns, picks up the half gone bale, and pushes it over the fence. It falls against the donkey's left front leg. The donkey steps back, looks quickly at Suzanne and then bends to the hay.

Suzanne stands for an hour, watching and listening, her right hand on the donkey's back; she can feel the heat of it, the broad muscles pulling. She can smell it too, the warm animalness of it.

At noon she leaves the donkey and walks out across the field. The field, about three acres, is a sloping corner of scrubby grass and weeds. Since she and Hillman bought the property ten years ago it's been left to its own design. Along one side is a row of birches, ash and alders. At the bottom is a stream. Suzanne walks to the far corner where an abandoned water trough sits in the brown bracken. She kicks it loose and begins dragging it back across the field. She gets three meters and stops. There are, in her way, mole hills and brambles and dried up thistles. It takes an hour. Finally, sweating and knee weary, she positions the trough against the fence. The donkey stares at her. The next hour is spent stretching a hose across the yard and filling the trough. The water is cloudy and leaf littered. The donkey takes a few quick sips, looks directly at Suzanne and gives out a low, shaky whinny.

2

Hillman Gazzard
c/o Refugee Crisis Centre
Calais, France
62100

Hilly —
Don't stop reading this letter. Don't put it down and think about something else and let whatever it is distract you from what you're doing right now. OK? What you're doing right now is you're reading this letter and it's important that you do that because I have something important to tell you.

I know you have a lot of things on your mind and that your mind is a crowded, busy place. I know that. But please. Just this once, stay with me.

I seem to have a visitor. A lodger. I have the very thing I never wanted. Other than you. I have someone with whom I'm sharing my space.

The visitor is a she and she is a donkey and she turned up out of nowhere and now stands staring at me from her favourite spot in the field in front of the house.

I know.

How many times did you ask? How many times did you beg me? Keep me awake at night, pressure me all day? You wanted animals. You wanted chickens and a dog and a peacock and maybe a horse. You wanted a population, a tribe. You wanted to feed things and water them and look after them and provide them with shelter. You wanted them to rely on you. While I refused. I know. I said: there's life enough here already. We're surrounded by it, dwarfed by it, swarmed on by it. I said: let it be enough.

One of the things about being here, as you know, is that I'm alone and that's mostly good and that's exactly the way I want it — I made things the way they are and it's OK but that doesn't mean that I don't, occasionally, miss you. Not often and not for long, but occasionally.

The donkey doesn't do much. Sticks close to the fence. Watches over me. Stands guard. I dragged over an old water trough for it. And Dorothy brought some hay.

Dorothy doesn't mention you. Your name won't sully her lips. She's loyal to me and that's that. She gives out no second chances. I will, tomorrow, stop in at the vets. And go to the library during lunch. See what I can learn about the inner workings of a donkey.

I've never before been much
interested in the inner workings of
anything. Not yours, not mine; not a
car, not a clock. Inner workings being
private places into which I seldom
venture.
    I'll let you know how we get on, my
visitor and me.

    S

3

Snow falls all night; in the morning the world is a
series of bumps and bulges. Suzanne peeks from
beneath the blanket and sees a corner of white. The
hedgerow, the laurel tree, the gate, the road; all are
hidden; a world without edges. She stands, pulls the
top blanket around her and hurries into the front
room. She tilts toward the window, squinting. The
donkey is still there, bedraggled and snow bothered,
clumps of frost clinging to its legs and back. It looks
at Suzanne with unblinking eyes.

    She dresses and goes to it, taking the blanket
with her. Preceded by tiny bursts of breathy cloud.
Pheasants scuttle away, struggling in the snow,
joining the rabbits and mice and those things that
keep their distance.

    She leads the donkey out of the pasture and
back across the yard, bringing it to the sheltered
strip between the house and garage. It isn't much
but it's clear. She rubs it all over, loosening and

removing the snow and ice. She covers it with the blanket, returns to the field and brings the remains of the hay bale. She fills a pail with water.

Better? She asks.

It sneezes and dips its head.

She gently rubs its ears.

What the hell do I call you? She asks.

What kind of name is that? was the first thing she ever said to Hillman.

My mother, said Hillman, had big ideas.

Hillman Gazzard? asked Suzanne. Is that what you said?

Hillman sighed and lowered his eyes. Suzanne measured out a meter of denim and watched his hands flutter across the counter top. It suits you, she said.

Does it?

Your mother knew what she was doing.

Hillman snorted and said, almost never.

Suzanne cut the denim, refolded the bolt, placed the fabric in a paper bag and said, I never met anyone named Hillman. Or Gazzard.

You've never met anyone like me, said Hillman.

I've met a lot of people.

Her eyes fully on him, unblinking.

He fingered the bag and said, no one like me.

She smiled and said, if you say so.

He gave her a five pound note, turned towards

the door and over his shoulder said, I say so.

He came the next day asking if she wanted to go out for lunch. He spoke with a schooled accent, neither too loud nor fast, as might a priest or a car salesman. What I am, he said, is I'm interested in you.

They sat in the park amongst school children and magpies, squirrels too and secretaries. On an uncomfortable bench by an oak tree. She ate her pasta while he sipped his tea. The thing you need to know about me, said Hillman, is simple.

Is it?

Sure it is.

He coughed and said, I'm a believer.

Two children, near the art gallery, were yelling something about an elephant.

A believer, repeated Suzanne.

That's right.

In what?

Good, said Hillman.

Suzanne replaced the lid of her plastic bowl and watched the magpies. There were three of them, each one identical to the other. Or so it seemed. With all the usual hopping and pecking. The children were discussing how much an elephant might weigh. More than a house, said one. Less than a boat, said the other. Without looking at Hillman she said, I have to get back.

She was suddenly and dully disappointed. What did she care about Christians or Buddhists or hippies or whatever kind of phantasist he was? With his good manners and his unclear eyes. His hair was not as she liked it, his nails were dirty, his shoes were cheap. He asked too many questions. And he believed in *good*. Whatever the hell that was.

She secures the blanket with an old length of rope and makes sure there's plenty of water and hay. She gives the donkey another long, all-over rub. She leans in close and blows warm air into its ears. She tells it: don't move. Stay here where it's sheltered. She goes inside and makes three phone calls, learning that horse blankets cost £50, a visit from a farrier costs £40, and small hay bales cost £5 each. Next she calls Dorothy.

I need a stable, she says. She can't stand outside.

No, says Dorothy. She can't.

I'm going to move her into the garage, says Suzanne. She'll be OK there. But –

Before Suzanne can say anything else Dorothy is yelling at Morris. Suzanne can hear a muffled conversation.

After a moment Dorothy returns and says, he'll be over next week. So long as the snow has cleared.

OK. That's great.

He'll buy some timber and let you know what it costs.

Fine.

And he'll bring the tractor. Clear a space for it to go.

Suzanne looks out the window at the empty field.

And Suze.

Yes?

Name it. You can't call it It forever.

The year they moved in Hillman arrived with a thirty year old Morris Minor; he built the garage around it. Three years later, when he bought a larger car, he removed the garage doors. There's no room inside for anything else. Suzanne enters sideways, sidling along the right wall. She backs the car out and parks it in front of the gate.

She places the hay bale and the water bucket inside, on the oil stained concrete. She coaxes in the donkey, whispering and encouraging, telling it to stay inside for the night. Make yourself at home, she says. If you need me I'm just next door.

The donkey's large, heavy head nudges against Suzanne. She strokes its nose, feeling the damp, snorting breath.

Hey girl, whispers Suzanne.

Hey, hey, hey.

Dusk settles. Small birds flutter in the shadows. The little bit of light that's left sits on the snow. Suzanne scratches the donkey behind its ears.

Now, now, she says.

4

Suzanne selects a plain brown blanket with black edging and three silver buckles. As she steps up to pay, the two women behind the counter stop talking. The redhead says, horse getting cold?

Suzanne shakes her head and says, donkey.

Ah, says the woman.

Said in a way that implies sympathy. As if having a donkey is slightly shameful. Slightly ridiculous. As if you can't afford or aren't yet ready for a horse. A horse being in every way superior. A horse being grownup and splendid.

Suzanne presents her card and the machine beeps. The woman says, pets can be a trial.

She uses the word pets as if talking to a child.

The blonde says, don't I know it. We got us a couple a rabbits last year and now what have we got?

The redhead waits.

Bloody rabbit colony.

Pests, says the redhead.

They each shake their heads sadly.

You need a gun is what you need.

They each nod.

I keep telling Charlie but he's too busy with his mates. Says Blondie. Shoot em all is what I say.

The rabbits? giggles the redhead, or his mates?

The over-lit shop is a chaos of garden tools and flower pots, axe handles and work clothes, boots and chicken wire, paints and bags of compost. Birdseed too and mouse traps. Along the back wall an array of ropes and chains and cords and wires.

My dad, says Blondie, is gonna come over and sort em out.

Oooohh daddy!

The redhead is pulling her hair down over her ears.

Says we should eat em.

The women giggle while Suzanne mumbles something that sounds like peadle.

Pardon?

People, says Suzanne.

The redhead does something with her nose and lips. Blondie shakes her head. Suzanne takes the blanket.

She hurries back to The Sewing Basket. The snow is mostly melted, gone to small clumps of blackened mush. At the side of the street are scraps of plastic and empty water bottles. A sky the colour of smoke. No breeze. The morning was slow, the afternoon slower. She calls a local farrier and arranges for him to come on the weekend. She also calls her neighbour, a farmer named Carwyn, and buys some hay. I'll stop by on the way home, she tells him.

That morning she'd called in at the library and

asked for a book about donkeys. The librarian had taken her to a section labelled Zoology, Pets, Animals (General).

What is it, the librarian had asked, that you're after?

When Suzanne didn't reply, the librarian pointed at different sections – history, picture books, practical care.

Care, I think, said Suzanne, uncertainly. Thinking: who cares for me?

She selected a book entitled *My Life With Donkeys, Their Everyday Ways*, by Bronwyn Hanley. It was a grim volume, published in 1958, bound in dull red canvas, dented and stained at the corners. On the first page was a donation stamp from the local college. It promised little.

Now, in the lessening light, she opens it and begins reading:

On all sides and in all corners we suffer. Children, hastily named and neglected, are mishandled. Factories, dark and fearsome, belch out those things least needed. Men with elaborate hats threaten each other. Wars, bombs, elections, treachery, starvation, disputed borders. But yet here they stand, warm and glad, nosing into the new grass and bracken. Ears trembling, tails swishing. To watch them now, on this May morning, to be here, is worth whatever sadnesses might later occur.

Donkeys require little of that which is ours to give. They are remarkably self-contained. Steady of temperament, good-natured, long suffering, companionable; a better walking partner would be difficult to imagine. And yet, at nearly every turn, we, in our wisdom, denigrate, ridicule and abuse these gentle friends.

Suzanne, taken by surprise, fingers the threadbare cover, searching for clues that might explain its strangeness. She flips to the last page and reads a brief biography of the author:

Bronwyn Hanley is a retired teacher, currently living with her small herd of donkeys in the hills of west Wales. Born in 1912, she grew up on a coastal small holding; she attended Cardiff University and spent time in Spain. For many years she taught English at Aberystwyth University. This is her first book.

Suzanne frowns and looks out the window. The streetlights have come on. A pregnant woman trudges by, pushing a stroller. It's neither dark nor dusk; the inbetween hour. She begins tidying the shop, preparing to shut things up. A car slushes slowly. The only sound, within and without, is a general and chronic hum, an electric mutter.

Hillman in June, twelve years ago, brought a clutch of damp weeds. Wild flowers, collected by the pathway. Sticks and leaves and blooms. Leaving her both confused and annoyed.

Do you, he asked, have a vase?

No, she said.

Meaning look around. This is a shop. A place of work. We sell fabric and zippers and cotton and upholstery foam. It's not somewhere you bring flowers to a stranger.

She pushed her tea cup across the counter and Hillman placed the limp flowers in it; it was a sorry display.

What is it, she asked, that you want?

Hillman hesitated. He clearly had no idea of what he wanted. He was, in that moment, for the first time, attractive. He looked at her with something approaching panic and might have fled had not Nora Stanley come in asking for tapestry thread.

Do you, asked Nora, have a six inch hoop and the same red silk I bought last week?

Suzanne found the hoop and thread and then, later, she was married.

5

Hillman Gazzard
c/o Refugee Crisis Centre
Calais, France
62100

Hilly —
The snow is upon us, creeping into
every holesome spot. What it is,
is everywhere. All day at uneven
intervals. I watch pheasants leave

behind three-pronged prints, pulling
themselves into the undergrowth. The
bird feeder is draped with tough
little customers, I want to knit them
each little coats. I imagine a posse
of puffed up dandies, each in a hand-
knitted cape and matching waistcoat.

I stand at the gate and wish for
rabbits. Their softened underbellies.
The warming look of them. The fields are
white splattered, the sky low. My feet
are cold.

As you know, I don't dream. I sleep.
I close my eyes and nothing happens.

I'm short and I'm thin but that's
fine — I never wanted to throw my weight
around.

I've been thinking of you and us and
how we got to be together and all the
things we did — cooking and laundry
and house painting and gardening and
planting trees —

Do you remember gathering apples
in October? Baked with blackberries.
A spoonful of currants too. And
elderberries.

Apples of an unknown variety.
Planted years before we arrived. In
exactly the wrong spot; they got no
light. Why were they planted there?
Under who's direction? The fruit they
produced was slight and not sweet.
Better left to the birds. Yellow,
small, brown marked, hard.

The birds too were yellow, small,

brown marked. They sat in the trees and pecked the apples. It was hard, sometimes, to distinguish between birds and apples. Sometimes, when the birds flew away, it was as if the apples had sprouted wings and discovered flight.

Remember how we'd grate two small apples and mix them with one large mashed potato? Add a pinch of salt, some caraway seeds and flour until the mixture stiffened. Chill for an hour. Push them into thin whitish patties and fry in olive oil...

And how we'd sit in front of the fire not talking, resting, being quiet?

I'm sitting here now, looking at the donkey, doing all this wondering.

S

6

I've made a list, she tells Dorothy.

Have you?

I have.

She holds up a piece of paper. Dorothy takes another biscuit. The biscuits, made by Dorothy, are a mess of ginger and raisins and hazelnuts and cherries; they give the impression of trying too hard.

Tell me the first five, says Dorothy.

Suzanne takes a deep breath and reads: Sheila, Goronwy, Caitlin, Nora, Rose.

Dorothy sighs and shakes her head.

Next.

Belle, May, Elsie, Gaynor, Felicity.

Suze, says Dorothy, she's a donkey, not your aunt.

Suzanne folds the paper and crumples it. She looks out the window at Morris. Dorothy squints and says, maybe try something a little less matronly.

Morris is sitting on a tractor, pushing dirt around. Suzanne can see the donkey, standing half in, half out of the garage. Without turning to Dorothy she says, you got any ideas?

The donkey's ears are pitched slightly forward, its eyes wide.

She's not mine, says Dorothy.

Nor mine.

Suzanne watches the donkey watching Morris. Morris scrapes a last corner of bare earth. The donkey tilts its head, pulls at a clump of hay and stamps the concrete with its tiny left front hoof. After another moment it raises its head, turns away and fills the afternoon with a mighty and contented braying.

The farrier runs his fingers along the donkey's knees and shanks, fetlocks and hocks, grasping the hoof and folding the leg back. The donkey seems uninterested.

The hooves look good, he says. No problems here.

He cleans out a few pebbles and some dirt, showing Suzanne how to do it. Then he clips the hooves and gives them a rub.

She's in good shape, he says.

He gently rubs her between her ears and says, aren't you girl?

He gathers his tools and says, what's her name?

Suzanne looks across the fields. There are birds out there of a medium size and shape. Clouds and an unseen moon. Bugs and beetles and innumerable mice and micclike creatures. Centipedes and worms and lice and slugs. The fields are full and lively of things unimaginable.

Gertrude. She says.

After dinner she sits on the sofa, reading the Bronwyn Hanley book.

I go walking with Antonio. Just the two of us, three miles to the coast and home again. I'm under no obligation to talk (although occasionally I do). We walk slowly, at an unhuman pace. A donkey pace. We stop often and investigate those things of interest to Antonio. They are not, usually, of interest to me. I fill my own time. Antonio snuffles around, nose down, while I wait. This enforced slowness is something for which I'm thankful.

I live in a place of wildness, of mistakes, of grass and rocks, of attempts, of almost. Also quiet, also digression. Contemplation too. I'm secret among the crags and hills and wind knocked trees. There was, until recently, no animal here bigger than I. I am the least brave, the least cunning; the most injurious.

I took in my first donkey seven years ago. A farmer had sold his farm; his animals were made homeless. A donkey came to me and I felt an immediate kinship. Over the next three years I acquired four more. Our herd, including myself, now stands at six. I am outnumbered. I provide them with space, with grass, with shelter, with water, with infrequent treats. I look after their hooves and teeth. When absolutely necessary I call a vet. They in turn provide me with a barrier between myself and the world of men. They ask no questions, their expectations are limited, they are fine and steady company.

We go walking on a strict rota. Each has its turn. Antonio then Margo then Rodrigo then Jess and finally Lindsay. We take one of a dozen footpaths; the neighbours are used to us. They wave and say hello. That funny old lady and her follies.

At the coast, in the car park, I tell the ocean hello. I admire its variable expanse, its unspeakable bigness. I have a chocolate bar. I have tea in a flask. Antonio lunches on sea kale. I remember a song my mother used to sing about gathering up seashells from the seashore, and about how (the song said) those were the happiest days of all.

Morris has sunk four six inch posts, driving each one a meter into the hard ground. Now he's nailing up braces. Suzanne holds one end of the timber and listens. He's wearing a thermal lined brown canvas overall. When he talks little gusts of steam surround his head. Tomorrow he'll nail on cedar cladding and put on a tin roof; one side will be left open. Morris, used to spending his time alone, talks ceaselessly in a baffling stream of unjoined sentences; he expects no answers.

I'm just saying, Morris says. Telling Suzanne about Aztecs and mustard gas and coal dust and vanished South American tribes.

Suzanne nods and says, sure.

As Morris thumps at a nail Suzanne turns and picks up the next brace.

We'll get some sun in a couple days, he says. Then turns and whispers, it turns out that Sheila's sister, the one that moved to Birmingham, the one with the hair, the short one, is basically a whore.

Poor Sheila, says Suzanne.

She heaves up the next brace.

There was a guy, says Morris, at the post office yesterday, kept repeating the word Bang! over and over. Then he slapped his documents on the counter and said, what kind of time do you call this then?

Suzanne nods and blows warm air on her hands. She enjoys being outside, being useful, having a precise course of action. And she likes Morris. He issues no demands; his hat, red wool, was knitted by Dorothy; he does those things he knows how to do. The fields are slick. Left over snow and ice is trickling into and over the earth. The wind is doing something in the trees.

In 1847, says Morris, in southern India, in July, thirty-seven children with the same name all died within three days of each other.

Suzanne frowns and nods.

Eventually, he says, the brambles win.

In the garage Suzanne strokes Gertrude's mane while Gertrude gently pushes into Suzanne's chest. There are, over the hill, three bright stars. A sliver of orange moon too, in the east.

You can go back to the field tomorrow, says Suzanne.

She looks out at the half built stable, at the cleared and trampled earth.

Move into your new stable.

Gertrude snorts out puffs of warm air. She pulls at some hay and chews it, waving her head from side to side.

You like that? asks Suzanne.

She crouches down and rubs Gertrude's legs; Gertrude makes a noise that involves teeth and lips.

I'll be having broth, says Suzanne. For my dinner. In a yellow bowl.

She talks just above a whisper; her hands are red and wind dried.

How does that sound?

Gertrude shuffles and wheezes.

Made with carrots and ginger and miso, barley floating around in there and slivered pepper. And after that a stewed apple. With yogurt.

Gertrude tears more hay.

I bought the bowl, says Suzanne, the yellow one, twelve years ago. When I first moved here. Back when I was just me.

She gives Gertrude one last brush with the curry comb and says, back before everything that happened happened.

7

Your problem, Cathy told her, is that you're just too quiet.

Suzanne, unaware that it was a problem, had nodded.

What I need is a people person.

Cathy had looked her up and down and sighed.

I need a go-getter. A real dynamo.

Suzanne wondered why she'd come. The ad had said: Wanted, shop assistant for part or full time work, references required, sewing skills helpful.

She had little or no sewing skills, no people skills, she'd never worked in a shop, she found it difficult to speak to strangers.

Talk to me, said Cathy.

Before Suzanne could reply Cathy said, the

sound of a person's voice is important.

The sound of my voice?

The timbre. The pitch. The voice, said Cathy, is the wellspring of authority.

Suzanne began to speak –

Don't whisper. Speak up.

I'm not whispering.

Charm me, said Cathy. Tell me what I need to know.

Suzanne stood, gathered her things and said, perhaps I made a mistake.

Now, now, said Cathy, throwing up her hands.

She advanced on Suzanne and said, don't get in a mood. One thing I can't stand is a mood.

Suzanne, who was not in a mood, who was wondering what, exactly, a mood was, stood silently.

You're not prone to moods, are you?

Cathy raised one eyebrow, did something with her left hand and said, because I can't tolerate moods. I have enough on my plate already without your moods.

From a large leather bag a purple silk scarf was withdrawn. She wrapped the scarf around her neck and said, I can't be doing with moods.

Suzanne made one last attempt. She looked slowly around the shop, turned to Cathy and said, I'm tidy.

The shop was heaped with unwound bolts of fabric, curtains, rolls of thread, netting, spools of cotton, flannel, unlabeled boxes and tangles of off-cuts.

Well, well, said Cathy. Little Miss Tidy Pants.

Suzanne nodded, Cathy smiled and that, it seemed, was enough. Suzanne was hired.

There's a Coast Guard helicopter overhead, whack-whacking east to west. Scuttling like a bug between clouds.

Suzanne tilts her head up and squints.

Not really like a bug at all. A bug being small and quiet and basically harmless. Keeping itself to itself. At home in forgotten corners. Brown and black and sometimes both, pushing between blades of grass, avoiding birds and badgers. While the helicopter roars. And spans great distances. And makes everyone aware of its presence. Painted bright red and silver. Gulping great portions of petrol and oil. An oppressive presence.

The day, towards evening, having calmed, becomes tomblike. Not a whisper, no murmur. In the realm of ataraxy. She takes a chair out to the stable and sits for a while. Ataraxy being a state of serene calmness. From the Greek *ataraxia*, from *a* *'not'* and *tarassein 'disturb'*. As in not disturbed. Nor interrupted. Nor even noticed.

Beside her Gertrude drowses. On the floor of the stable a thick layer of straw has been scattered. Earlier Gertrude had spent the afternoon parading across the pasture, nosing its boundaries, nibbling at what greenery remained. She then came into the stable, laid on her back, hooves aloft, and rolled in the fresh hay.

The last light leaves. Gertrude, in her new blanket, snuffles. The cold, at night, is colder. The trees, along the stream, are less like trees. The fields are dark slopes. All is melded together. The moon charcoals the world. It's changed into a foreign place where night animals get busy. Where stars and bats and badgers lurk around. Suzanne leans forward, as if to leave, then sits back. In her mumbling fashion she sighs and says something about the mud.

That's what we'll get now. Weeks of mud.

Gertrude pays no mind.

I wasn't like this immediately, says Suzanne. It took time.

We each got to do our own fair share. Is what Hillman used to tell her.

Our own fair share?

Yes.

Over breakfast he was so serious.

To make things better, he said.

Things?

Yes.

Better?

Absolutely.

What things and for whom?

He worked with an organisation that rehoused the homeless. He talked often and at length about shifting social imperatives and the need for a national housing strategy.

Shelter, he said, is the least a civilised society can provide.

Suzanne had wondered about the word civilised.

The *very* least, Hillman had said.

People, homeless or otherwise, in need or otherwise, were, to Suzanne, a puzzlement. She felt of no use to them nor they to her. It was as if a trick had been played, a mistake; she felt no kindredness, no connection, no allegiance. She often wondered: to whom am I related?

Hillman often disappeared into the darker corners of dishevelled cities, distributing blankets and protein bars, donated mittens and bottles of water. He returned exhausted, overwhelmed with purpose and frustration.

We must, he said, do all we can.

Suzanne, wide eyed, bewildered, did nothing.

One of the things that happened back then was that Cathy got ill, began to lose weight, developed kidney problems, turned a ghostly shade of yellow, and there it was; cancer. Her illness and its consequences were never discussed. She was given six months to live and lasted three. The shop was bequeathed to a distant cousin; the cousin never visited. Suzanne continued as before, ordering stock and paying invoices, filing VAT returns, paying rates and taxes. She repainted the interior walls, bought a new rug and radio, hung a picture of an autumnal river scene. The shop, under Suzanne's hand, was tidy and dependable; Suzanne herself was mostly overlooked. A small rent was paid to the distant cousin.

Her job relied on those qualities at which she least excelled. She had no interest in people's distractions, in the things they bought and worked for, their holidays and children, their ills and disappointments. She had no small talk. She sat quietly and apart; some women, away from the shop, whispered that she might be simple. Where Cathy had forged a specific relationship with each of her customers, Suzanne struggled to remember names. There were so many of them. And they all acted so strangely. Bustling about importantly, intent on some errand, sure of their place in the world. She remembered faces, and orders, but never names. And they insisted on changing their hairstyles; they wore a dizzying array of outfits; they had children and grandchildren and dogs and husbands. It was impossible; Suzanne gave up and treated each one with the same hushed patience.

People want to like you, Cathy had once told her, but they have to be reminded.

Suzanne failed to remind anyone of anything.

You have to master, Cathy said, the jocular

approach. Women like a bit of fussing.

Suzanne had mastered nothing. She was not confident, she was not enthusiastic, she was neither cheerful nor jolly. Her hair wasn't correct, her clothes were off center. Neither was she unhappy or angry; she was simply not what the world expected her to be.

It's not difficult, on the internet, to find a cheap copy of the Bronwyn Hanley book. She orders it and feels like she's done something good. She makes dinner and it's quiet and she listens to the wind for awhile and then she moves into the front room and turns on the TV. She finds a movie about young detectives with complicated private lives. The detectives are all extremely pretty and live in large flats that overlook a river. The flats contain furniture made from steel and glass. They rush around frantically shouting and drinking and being chased and shooting. One of them is captured and locked in a toilet. Doors are kicked in, cars are stolen; there's much blood and loud music. Suzanne watches for an hour and then turns it off.

In the morning the snow has mostly melted, leaving white droppings that drift around the pasture. Mud between them. Little else, no crocuses yet, no dandelions, no red clover, no poppies, no primrose.

She finds a dead robin at the foot of a sycamore tree. Still limp; she nudges it with her shoe. Still bright, a knot of rusted fluff. She looks across the field at the wetted grass, at the leafless trees, at the mossy rocks and stones. And in the center of it the stable. And Gertrude.

APRIL

Spring comes with all it's new business. Suzanne stands in the pasture and looks at the green beginnings. It's still cold, the early sun doing its weak thing. There were high winds all night and she hasn't slept. Twigs and small branches lay scattered across the field. Gertrude nuzzles into Suzanne and the day is silver.

A woman came in the shop yesterday, says Suzanne, collecting for charity.

A breeze nudges Gertrude's mane.

Suzanne looks down and says, I told her I'd already donated my husband.

Gertrude investigates a clump of something yellow. Almost yellow. Something green that's turning yellow. That will be, in another week, only yellow. Suzanne leans back against a fence post. There are no clouds. A crow caws.

She waits for Gertrude to move on. They've walked out of the pasture and to the west, across a neighbor's field and onto a bridleway. They'll walk to a nearby lake, sit for as long as Gertrude wants to sit, and then walk back. Across the hill they can hear the sputtering wheeze of a tractor. Gertrude wears a halter; attached to it is a length of plaited canvas. Suzanne, waiting for Gertrude, holds the lead loosely. There's no point hurrying or pressing; Gertrude walks at her own erratic pace.

The day had started clear. Sun came slowly across the garden, in an uneven block, lighting the edges of the dogwood and the sedum. The deflowered rhododendron too. The pink and purple heathers and the twisted willow. The wind, last night, was the kind that knows no borders. Pushing at windows, demanding to be noticed, to be feared perhaps, to be acknowledged. Deranged, yelping across the yard.

Bloody wind, Suzanne had whispered. Go away and settle down.

Safe in bed. Out of harms way. In her t-shirt and thick socks. Warm and blanketed and not in need of a piss. With only the wind to irk her.

They walk up a rise, slowly. Alongside the fields where rabbits and pheasants wait. Then scatter. There is, by the side of the lane, an oak tree that's split. Perhaps struck by lightening, perhaps rotten from the inside out; it sprawls across the field. They continue up further still, to the empty places where something is always dead. Last week a sheep; today a crow. Once, last spring, a fox. They walk until they stop walking and then they stand for a while watching rabbits and pheasants and smelling whatever animal is no longer.

At the side of the lake Gertrude grazes while Suzanne reads Bronwyn Hanley.

My loneliness has, at times, been large. It has roosted upon my shoulders, nested in my hair, perched on my head. My donkeys daily show me a different way. When Chuang Tzu wrote the following paragraphs, in the fourth century, he could have been writing about donkeys:

"The true man of old did not fight against poverty, nor did he look for fulfillment through riches – for he had no grand plans. Therefore, he never regretted any failure, nor exulted in success. He could scale the heights without fear, plumb the depths without difficulties, and go through fire without pain. This is the kind of person whose understanding has lifted him towards the Tao.

The true man of old did not hold on to life, nor did he fear death. He arrived without expectation and left without resistance. He went calmly, he came calmly and that was that."

My donkeys care for only that which is most simple. They are neither vain nor greedy nor petty nor mean. They are not highbred race horses or strutting show stallions; they are not preening prize winners. They are lowly and decent. They humble me.

My filth fingered brother, says Dorothy, five foot two in his muddied boots, has never in his life, never once, seen the ocean.

Suzanne nods. Dorothy shares ownership of her farm with her brother. Whom she despises. He lives

49

twenty miles away in a newly built manor house.

No imagination, says Dorothy. Not a bit of it. Just sits there in his tweeds being dull.

She sighs theatrically and closes her eyes. Morris's father had died last month, having spent the last year of his life in Manchester, in pubs and on park benches, drinking his pension. The end had come grimly, in a bed sit. Debts, affairs, booze, gambling; he fell in with a bad crowd and got nixed.

Those people, Dorothy said at the time, eat people like gramps for breakfast.

By 'those people' she means people who live in the city. Dorothy has no time for city folk. She blames them for all the ills of the world; global warming, the decline in personal grooming and manners, the slide into fiscal chaos, the cheapening of social life, the unpredictability of the weather.

I'm just saying that they're different. She once said. In intent and smell. Clothes too and the use of condiments.

The tea is cold. Suzanne, after her walk, is tired. She listens to Dorothy as she might listen to the stream or to the wind. She pulls her feet up onto the sofa and tries to say something. It comes out a breathy mumble. Dorothy grimaces and calls her brother a vile plum.

She says this as if she's angry.

Suzanne tells her that perhaps he's neither good nor bad. That maybe he just is what he is.

That's what you always say about everything.

That's what I always think about everything.
But it gets me nowhere.

It gets you here, says Suzanne, indicating the
empty fields, the house, the rabbits, the near blue
sky.

Morris, says Dorothy, was taking his afternoon
nap when I left. Snoring like a chainsaw.

Then she says something about her car and a
leaky radiator that Suzanne can't quite make out.
Suzanne offers more tea which Dorothy refuses.
Dorothy complains, at length, about the main-
tenance of local gutters, drains and roads. She
supplies locations, dates and names. She bemoans
the ability of council workers to do a simple job
properly. Likewise the lack of funds and where
they're spent. Also their insistence on cutting the
hedges too early. In this mumbled way they spend
an hour.

2

Hillman Gazzard
c/o EU Migration Aid Agency
Kos, Greece
85302

Hilly —
I guess I've made it through another
winter.
   We each have our victories.

Yours include distributing food, aid and shelter to streams of dehoused and displaced families.

Mine include getting out of bed.

Dorothy and Morris pester me. They're each admired and I'm thankful for them but I tell them that my loneliness has nothing to do with lack of company.

A concept they don't fully grasp.

I spend what time I can with Gertrude. Do you know the Geraint Goodwin quote: ...the knowledgeless companionship of the earth.

That nearly says something about how I feel.

You know how it is with me. I'm broken in a very specific way. A way that has to do with me and only me and no one else. I'm a stranger to every other person I've ever met. My loneliness is my own. I made it.

I hope you're busy and your hands are needed.

The ash tree near the stream is looking rough. Sores have opened on its trunk. I'll check its leaves, when they come, for disease.

The stream is up — another rainy night and it'll overflow its banks.

The roof, above the back door, still leaks.

While you're doing your good works I'm sitting and standing and walking around with Gertrude. We are two

sisters who whisper in the evening.
Of the kind who have no children or
nephews. Who spend their time quietly
signalling each other. Who appear
undernourished but content. We are,
together, singular.
    Separate.
    There are mice here who remember
you. They ask about you. Is he well?
Still handsome? Still gentle and
without an angry bone in his body?
Still doing his best to save us all? I
tell them yes, thank you for asking,
I'm sure he is.
    I'm sure you are —

    S

3

Suzanne worries about Gertrude's aloneness.
Donkeys, she's told, are a herd animal, they choose,
in the wild, to live with others of their own kind.
The same, she thinks, can and has been said about
humans. Things, true and otherwise, are being said
all the time. People loving to talk and to listen to
themselves talk. Gertrude doesn't seem unwell. She
shows no signs of melancholia. She eats, she sleeps
well, she treats Suzanne with something that feels
like affection. Her coat and teeth are healthy, her
eyes bright. And yet Suzanne wonders if she wants
companionship of an equine nature.

    She asks Dorothy to bring over a small horse

so they can see how Gertrude reacts.

In the winter Gertrude preferred grain to hay, the grain being richer; now, with the weather coming milder, she sticks to hay and grass. She knows what she wants. She knows what's good for her. She knows, in a way that has always escaped Suzanne, who she is. Suzanne notices that she eats differently in the morning, searching out specific plants and grasses. There was a time, last month, when she looked sluggish. She found a clump of new nettles and, for three days, ate very little else. She looked better immediately.

The recent rain has swollen the stream. The brown water is frantic, carrying large sticks, feathers, leaves and branches. A hat swishes by. Of the kind given away to farmers, red and white with a dark peak. A logo of some description on the front.

In the evening she sits in the front room, radioless, TVless, one table lamp on. The residue of her life, her entire life, here in this room. Papers, files from the shop, bills, books; in one envelope a handful of photographs. Two of her mother. One of herself as a child. Likewise, one of Hilly as a child. (Hilly smiling; Suzanne scowling.) One of the house in which she was born. One, taken by Hilly, of a ruined barn two miles down the road. One of a childhood cat. One of Hilly and she getting married. Another of them on a beach. One, strangely, of an empty bus shelter. The envelope is labeled Miseries.

(Concerning the yellow overhead light: it was there when they moved in. An antique glass bauble that attracts spiders; it's now filled with their dead and dusted bodies; they gather in darkened clumps; she hasn't the heart to throw them out.)

She had a mother, a woman of inexact desires, and a father who died young. There were cousins of a distant variety; an uncle in Australia. She was once shown pictures, told stories by her mother. At no point did they cause her to feel a part of anything.

She remembers her mother's end: the slow damage and collapse, the unwillingness, the anger, the remorse, the being and staying gone. The organisation and lack thereof. The wanting. The surprise, surprise.

Outside it's very empty. Which means that here, in the hills, in the uplands, away from the thrust of citidom, inhabitants are required, if needed, to invent their own communities. Communities that include sycamores and dog woods and pheasants and stony outcroppings and wood pigeons; those things that jumble together. Those things which have no other community.

In the morning she brushes Gertrude. She tells her a few things. Things like how badly she slept and how it's getting lighter in the mornings and how later Dorothy is bringing over a pony. Then for a while she's quiet. The morning rattles. The sky is dark and grey and wet and low. Then she says something about the news she heard last night on the radio.

She looks down the hill and across the stream.

Always the same. She says.

She strokes Gertrude's mane, her forelock, the tufts that crown her ears.

An assumption that we can solve all our problems by killing things.

She pulls the comb through the mane.

Everything is expendable. She says. Everything that isn't rich and fat and white and powerful.

She leans forward and smells Gertrude's coat. She rests her forehead on Gertrude's back. She can hear the rumblings of Gertrude's stomach. She stands, crosses the stable, picks up a pair of scissors and cuts the twine on a bale of hay.

Dorothy stands beside the horse trailer and says, Madam loves a ride.

Meaning the pony.

She nods at the trailer and says, likes to be chauffeured. See the sights, let the breeze get at her hair.

She opens the trailer, pulls out the ramp and says, Madam decided, this morning, that her mane needed a comb and trim.

Madam needs no coaxing. She steps slowly down the ramp, away from the trailer, bends to the grass and begins grazing. She's a Dartmoor pony, roughly the same age and size as Gertrude.

Dorothy rolls her eyes and says, can't go visiting without a trip to the hairdresser.

Suzanne approaches Madam. She makes a cooing noise and gently strokes Madam's flank.

Morris, says Dorothy, has gone walking. In a huff. We had a disagreement.

Suzanne, who isn't listening, nods.

Ask anyone, says Dorothy. My sense of justice is well known.

Madam straightens and looks across the yard. Gertrude, at the fence, ears high, stares back.

If something's not fair, says Dorothy, it rankles me. I get rankled.

Madam starts across the yard.

It's just the way I'm built.

Suzanne follows as Madam heads straight for Gertrude.

I told Morris that it's just not fair and there's no amount of arguing that can make it different. There's more than one kind of people in this world and that's a fact.

As Madam approaches the fence Gertrude turns away. She trots quickly across the pasture, putting

as much space as possible between herself and
Madam. Suzanne opens the gate and Madam steps
into the field. On the far side, near the birches and
alders, Gertrude watches.

I tell Morris, says Dorothy, that I won't set
out to harm, nor make any move for gain. It just
isn't me.

Suzanne stands at the gate. Gertrude keeps
to the edges of the pasture; Madam advances,
Gertrude retreats.

I don't consider a plumber as lowly, says
Dorothy. Why should I? I won't barter for riches.

Gertrude and Madam circle the field. When one
stops so does the other. There is, between them, a
slope of new grass, dotted with mole hills; birds of
a medium size fill the trees.

Suzanne crosses to Gertrude and strokes her
nose.

Whassamadda? She whispers.

The whole of Gertrude is aquiver, she pushes
into Suzanne, her ears are pitched forward, her
eyes are wide, there is about her a peculiar odour.

Don't you want to meet Madam?

Gertrude stamps her hooves into the soft earth.
When Madam approaches Gertrude sucks in air
and trembles. She plants her hooves and bares her
teeth. Suzanne turns and herds Madam back across
the field and out the gate. When the gate is bolted
Gertrude lets out a triumphant bray.

What Morris better do, Dorothy says, is be a little less definitive.

Suzanne is thinking about the way Morris once said, seems like the whole world is filling up with women.

Gertrude is a solitaire. She says.

While Madam likes a party. Says Dorothy.

Suzanne looks across the table, across the room, out the window and across the field at the distant hills where pastures get mixed up with trees and streams and gated lanes. She can see, barely, farm-yards and hedgerows out there and the people and animals that move among them. Uneven green parcels of land, divided and chopped. Behind her house it's wilder, more open, little fenced, a less broken stretch of upland. Farmers claim it's mostly worthless. No good for crops, or hay, or cattle. Only thing worth having up there is sheep, they say. While Suzanne's untended acres rush with rabbits and foxes and pheasants and mice and ferns and moss and thistles and dock weed and all manner of low quality, inferior things. Herself included.

Dorothy sits back and says, don't cling to your own ideas. That's my advice. What is little and what is much are terms of very limited use.

Suzanne nods, still looking outside. There are sheep and cattle out there. Horses too. Dogs the colour of mud. With white faces. A dull sun. Green shoots on the dogwood. A pitchfork and three metres of rope. A shovel leaning against the garage.

The pale tops of daffodils. And somewhere a truck of the kind with four wheel drive. That sputters and spits. She listens as it fades into the distance.

4

The rain comes unexpectedly, from the east. One moment a pale grey sky and then suddenly a down pour. Suzanne is at the gate, watching rabbits. There are a dozen out there sitting in the grass. Go, go, go, she whispers. Go away and be dry.

The rain angles across the ridge.

Gravel and boulders and willow trees, remain as you were. She says. Be stationary and get wet.

There are rooted things and there are mobile things. Some run, some don't.

Across the valley is the quarry. Trucks come and go in the grey fog. On a clear day you can see the tiny trucks and the tiny men who drive them pushing huge piles of gravel around. Today Suzanne can only hear them; crunching and shifting gears, shouting instructions, beeping horns.

The quarrymen cut and bomb the hills, leaving all the inside layers exposed. Grey guts. It's a fearsome, brutal business. They use dynamite and huge toothed machines. The quarrymen wear large boots and hard hats. They shout affectionate nicknames at each other. The nicknames often involve body parts and nationalities. Later, the cut and bombed bits are pushed into machines, crushed into gravel, and then graded into different sizes. Every few years Suzanne arranges for a load of crushed guts to be brought here, to her lane, to the place where she's now standing.

Here I am, she says to herself, waiting, a woman of a certain age, watching rabbits.

The gravel should arrive any minute. The foreman called twenty minutes ago and said the truck was leaving the yard.

Seven tonnes of grey guts, dumped in piles along the lane. That Suzanne will then spread with a shovel and rake. Filling pot holes and gullies. A shovel load at a time. Until everything is level. At which point she'll stamp, stamp, stamp it down. Tormenting both her back and her boots. It will take all afternoon, allowing for tea breaks and the occasional rain shower; at dusk she'll limp home and without changing clothes fall asleep on the sofa.

She watches three rabbits sitting together in a pale cluster, like a circle of mushrooms. Noses in the cool, silaged air. Behind them is a field of trees that she and Hillman planted seven years ago. Oak. Hazel. Alder. Blackthorne. Apple. Willow. Rowan. Ash. Sycamore. Birch. Holly. Elder. How often has she pulled, from around their roots, the worst of the bracken, the sea grass, the dock weeds, the thistles? How many stakes and guards has she replaced? How many dead limbs has she removed? How often has she stood, in the morning, measuring their progress? Our Field Of Maybe, is what Hillman called it.

In the evening, immobilized with fatigue, she sits on the sofa with a hot water bottle and watches the stable. Only Gertrude's head is visible. It's a comfort, to see her rounded nose and tall ears, to imagine the hard and soft feel of it. She wonders what thoughts the head might hold. She looks around the room and wonders what thoughts her own head might hold. Her shoulders, her back, her knees and elbows, everything is feeble with exhaustion. Time, which is not constant, blurs. Suzanne is quiet and the room is quiet. The wind and the bats and a hundred other unseen night-time things aren't, but Suzanne is. She stretches out on the sofa. Her feet point at the ceiling. Her mind circles the room. She feels a little bit dead. How has she managed to live here, alone, all these years? It feels like an act of monumental will from a person who has very little will at all, let alone anything monumental. People like me, she tells herself, should never live alone. She gazes up at the shadowed ceiling and tells herself, people like me can only live alone. She doesn't eat and she doesn't change clothes and she doesn't turn on the light. She rearranges the hot water bottle and closes her eyes. We shouldn't be expected to mix with other people; we have our silences and little deaths and our monumental wills and they have their families and Sunday roasts and trips to Blackpool. How can we be expected to make sense of each other? How can we be expected to share the same planet?

In the morning she opens the gate and lets Gertrude wander into the yard. She bends to a rose bush that was bought the year they moved in. They bought the flowering currant a year later. The twisted hazel and ornamental dogwood the summer after that. They bought things and planted them and in the winter mulched them and often fed and watered them and they mostly grew.

Gertrude stands patiently near the garage.

I'm not sure what it all means, Suzanne says.

Gertrude says nothing.

We spent a lot of time weeding, says Suzanne. And watching the things we'd planted and doing what was necessary to keep them healthy. And slowly it became more me than Hilly but I didn't mind. Hilly got bored with plants and needed people and he sought them out and was better amongst them. I was better here.

Gertrude shuffles around and blows out air. Suzanne snips off a broken branch.

Hilly, says Suzanne, had a big need for helping. While I had none. I didn't care for news or gossip or the Royal family, for wars or whatever airplanes were fashionable. I just bumped along, seeing to my own limited needs and not hurting anyone else. Or so I like to tell myself.

Gertrude does her nuzzling into the undergrowth. Now and then she sneezes. The morning
is without urgency. There are flies buzzing and bees
too and there are a few leaves up on the ash tree.

I can just about be here like this. Says Suzanne.

5

```
Hillman Gazzard
c/o EU Migration Aid Agency
Kos, Greece
85302
```

```
Hilly —

Do you still favour a boot? Of the old
fashioned variety? Leather with long
laces and many eyelets? I still have
the ones I bought when we first met. The
soles are worn, the laces loose, the
edges cracked; no longer do they keep
out either the wet or the cold. Mostly
they remind me of other, drier, less
hasty walks.
    I can, this morning, see what? Ten,
twenty feet, no more. The birch, the
wheel barrow, the pathway through the
bracken, all gone. The fog flows and
settles while I sit unmoving at the
window.
    I can hear the squeak of bats, the
random flap of their wings. The dash too
of wind.
```

I have nothing of import to tell
you.
    I never did.
    I often thought: what can I tell
you?
    I looked for words but words failed.
I was mostly silent and I tried to
apologize but I found it difficult to
find the words for even that. You used
to say, talk to me and I used to think:
what can I say? I have no words.
    Gertrude has a morning routine.
When I wake she's in the most easterly
corner of the field. I stand in the
kitchen and watch. She slowly circles
the pasture, sticking to the fence,
nosing around, grazing. An entire
circuit takes two hours. She then moves
over to the centre of the pasture and
stays there for a bit. Then it's back
to the stable and a roll in the hay.
All the while sneezing and braying and
dropping piles of poo.
    I'm sure your mornings are filled
with things of which I can't begin to
imagine. I picture you and a room (a
field? a boat? an expanse) of hungry and
desperate refugees, people who have
had their lives and stories stolen,
and I'm so overwhelmed I cease to be.
What kind of world is this? I evaporate
in a cloud of fevered anxiousness. I
force myself to sit down, turn off the
lights, take deep breaths and think
of Gertrude. In this way, slowly, I'm

returned to myself.

Whoever that is.

You can see that I have no business being anywhere but here. You always knew that. Ill equipped me.

I wish you whatever it is that would do you the most good.

Yours

S

6

I was there, in the mid morning, secreted behind an olive tree. The air was yellowy with sage and thyme. I was wearing a dress made of Egyptian cotton, wide at the neck and loose around my knees. On my feet were sandals with blue rope soles. My hair was clipped close. How brown I was, how yellow the day! How far from green Wales! I crouched lower with my binoculars and my writing pad. Before me a small herd of donkeys were interacting in delicate and precise ways. I had in mind to write about these quiet and gentle animals. Observation, I thought, was a good starting point.

I was young and without experience. All I knew of donkeys came from the pages of Don Quixote. I took a copy with me and, amongst the wild herbs and turtles, reacquainted myself with it. The relationship between Sancho and his donkey Dapple affected me deeply. I read over and over again the passage where Sancho says of Dapple: "How hast

*thou been, my dear Dapple, my trusty companion
and joy of my eyes!" I read too how he told Dapple:
"Oh what unexpected accidents, which at every
turn befall those who live in this miserable world!"*

*I was in possession of paper, pencils, time and,
in a grey metal flask, tea. I went each morning for
two weeks, setting up house in the olive grove. I
learned that I knew nothing. I learned that knowing
nothing is a good position from which to begin. I
watched and I took notes.*

*Each adult donkey seemed to have a definite
range, depending on the availability of food and
water. The donkeys spent half their time looking
for food and water, the other half in quiet relax-
ation. At all times one donkey remained on guard.
Donkeys, when they sensed danger, invariably stood
and faced their foe. Horses fled.*

*The ears of a donkey are a window to its being.
Watch the guard donkey's ears – they stand and fall
and quiver and twist; they resemble a furred radar.*

*Donkeys possess the largest of all equine ears; if
equine ears are one of the primary portals through
which horses and donkeys perceive the world, then
donkeys possess the most subtle equipment available.*

*In donkey communities the newly born are
protected, food is shared, predators are dealt with
collectively. The days are spent in search of food,
water and companionship; an air of grace and
tranquility prevails.*

This is not, let's be frank, what we find in most

human communities. The young are not protected,
food is not shared; individuals are left alone to defend
themselves against intruders. Grace and tranquility
do not rule. In this, in the simple act of being alive,
donkeys are unquestionably our superiors.

Suzanne in The Sewing Basket, door open to the day, the sun just above the Co-op, watches two young women finger bolts of bright fleece. One of them, in white, tells the other, his mum's coming over tonight and I told him I'm not cooking for *her*.

She picks up another bolt and says, bitch.

The other woman, with short blue hair, says, whatyagonnadothen?

Kentucky Fried Chicken. I spoze.

Oh great. I love a nice Kentucky.

The first woman purrs and says, everybody wins.

After dinner in the darkening kitchen Suzanne answers the telephone. My brother arrives tomorrow, is what she hears.

She sits on the old church chair Hillman bought the first winter they were married.

Dorothy sighs and says, the cow handed bastard.

Before Suzanne can say anything, Dorothy says, he's so wrong about everything and he's dumb too and I can't stand to have him here.

Oh dear. Says Suzanne.

He's on his way north, says Dorothy. Where he's going to kill things. He's stopping here overnight.

Oh dear. Says Suzanne.

And of course Morris hates him just as much as I do so it's not going to be any fun. Morris infuriates him. He shouts at him and Morris gets flustered and makes even less sense than usual.

Suzanne tries to think of something to say.

Are you there? asks Dorothy.

Maybe you could come over here, says Suzanne. Leave him there alone. I could invent an emergency.

He'd only insist on coming with me.

Suzanne feels her chest tighten and Dorothy says, I couldn't do that to you.

Well –

He's going on a hunting trip. Killing birds. On an estate somewhere. With other brain-dead bullies. Dressed up in their tweeds and boots and stupid fucking hats. Drink whiskey all night and smoke cigars and wander around half cocked shooting at anything that moves. Country thugs.

Family, says Suzanne.

Which you don't have, says Dorothy. Lucky you.

Suzanne can hear Morris in the background.

Morris, says Dorothy, says to tell you that he found a complete fox skeleton yesterday.

Suzanne looks out at the night unlit by stars. She hasn't yet turned on any lights.

And that you can have the skull. Which he seems to think is something you want.

Tell him thank you. Says Suzanne.

She can hear Morris saying something else.

He also says that yesterday in town he heard someone say that the Queen died in 1968 and that for fifty years an actress by the name of Geraldine Jackson has been playing the part. Which he also seems to think you need to know.

Suzanne smiles and says, yes. I do. Thanks.

There is, over Gertrude's stable, a single flickering star. Of the kind that has a name, that has a number, that's part of a constellation. There are rooms of people somewhere, earnest men and women, who map and name the heavens. They give each star a name, a grid marking, they compile charts, they write books, they analyze and record data; they send machines out to move amongst them. They teach in universities, they have the lives they have, they are mostly paid well for doing the thing they love, they are admired and notable.

When Suzanne closes her eyes the star is gone.

There was the time that Hillman asked her if she knew how many children died of neglect in the UK.

How many homeless people died of exposure?

How many teenagers are stabbed to death?

How many young women were attacked and raped?

How many elderly people died alone?

He recited these statistics in a melancholy sing song, his voice barely above a whisper. He held her hand. He tried, in his way, to involve her. He asked her to go on marches, on demonstrations, to volunteer at shelters, to hand out free shoes on the streets of Walsall. She declined.

I'll stay here, she said, with the finches and the moss.

Where you're comfortable.

She gave him the blank stare and said, have I ever been comfortable?

But –

She held up her hand and told him, people die. It happens.

He recited Ghandi at her. Something about the preciousness of all human life. She mumbled something he couldn't hear. Something about human life not being precious. She looked away from his stricken eyes.

Or no more so than any other life. She said. The life of a cat or a cow or an oak tree or a crow or some burdock.

She looked out at the creeping dark and said something about how if all life was equally precious then that meant that nothing was precious.

But –

The best option...

Suzanne sat in the church chair and examined her feet.

…is indifference.

They were both quiet for a minute as Hillman crossed the room.

The oak tree, said Suzanne, is indifferent to the rabbit. The crow is indifferent to the grass.

Hillman's silhouette filled the window.

Let others be what they are. Be a noninfluencer.

But don't you want to influence the world? Make it better?

Have we ever? Have we ever made anything better?

We can try.

I want the world to be free of our constant meddling.

Is that what I do? Meddle?

You repair the results of meddling. You meddle with the meddling.

Ridiculous.

Maybe. Said Suzanne.

Certainly. Said Hillman.

You're a good man. She said.

Am I?

You're constantly you.

He didn't reply. He stood at the window watching nothing. There was a lot of it out there. It was slow and it was tall and it was dark and it was deep. It crept up and surrounded the house. It sat on the hills and blew through the trees. It was everything. He stood there long after Suzanne had left the room.

JULY

There are drifts of yellow flowers here. Tiny, barely taller than the grass that surround them. They push up over the grass to get some sun. To get food. To get that which they need in order to live. They aren't dandelions. Nor primroses. They're tiny yellow flowers that must have a name. Maybe you know what they're called. You always knew that sort of thing. You bought books about flowers and trees and native shrubs. Books that you carried with you on our walks.

You can't see these flowers now because you're not here. You're someplace else. In the middle east now. On the Syrian border.

I'm here. Gertrude's here.

You used to tell me their names and I never listened.

Birds too.

Blackcap, you'd say. Red billed chough. Starling. Checking them against the pictures in your book.

To me they were That One Over There or The One With A Tail That's Shaped Like A V or The Ones With Yellow Petals or The Grey One Who's Terribly Shy. I didn't want to saddle them with names.

Who are we to tell birds and flowers who they are?

Gertrude doesn't eat the yellow flowers. She delicately pushes them aside and sticks to the leafier green stuff.

I've spent the past three nights in the stable. I've set up a cot in the corner. For two weeks I can do as I please; the shop closed for my summer break. Two weeks of not leaving the house, the yard, the fields. Why would I go to France? To Ibiza? To Spain? What's in Spain? Sancho and Dapple are long gone. It's all cars and shops and new shoes and films and tiny phones and music I don't understand. Who am I that I need to be always on the move? Do I need to see the sea? Is there anything so important it means I should leave my home?

I want, in some small way, to see the world as Gertrude sees it. Is that possible? Am I allowed that? Get down on her level and be obstinate.

A question of angles.

Last night, sleeping on my cot, feeling the heat of her snuffling, listening to random night pops and creaks, the owls, the wind, I felt more than ever a ghost in my own life. The master of the silent stare; the enemy of restlessness. I don't want to rest less; I want, if anything, to rest more. The world, that part of it we've created, is overrated. My desire is to exist in a manner that makes experience irrelevant. No stories, no past deeds, no intentions, no expectations, no history.

The Friday before I closed the shop a woman came in wearing a t-shirt that said Do Epic Shit.

I closed the shop three hours early and fled home to Gertrude.

Who are we to Do Epic Shit? Surely that's the mistake we've always made. Doing Epic Shit. Can we not Do Less Epic Shit? Can we not, perhaps, do nothing at all? Where has all this Epic Doing gotten us? In a great bloody Epic Mess is where. One person does some Epic Shit and the next person has to do some Epic Shit Fixing. What kind of person believes that the Epic Shit they're doing is going to be anything other than an Epic Shit Disaster? Why must we always think on an epic scale? To invent the train is also to invent the train wreck. Who are we to presume we're capable of an Epic Victory? A victory in which no one suffers. Why can we not Do Tiny Shit? Do the Tiniest Shit imaginable. Do things so small it seems we're doing nothing. Practice breathing. Practice watching. Practice sitting quietly. Do those things for twenty years and then maybe, just maybe, you can move on and do some talking. Using small words of no more than two syllables. Composed mostly in questions. Try that for five years and then maybe, just maybe, you can move on to some walking around. And that, frankly, given our past record, should be all we're allowed. Like sheep, like cows. No tools, no fire, no wheels, no iron. The entire spectrum of human endeavour should be breathing, sitting, walking around and asking questions. Full stop. Finished.

Hillman knew. He tried, in his way, to tell me. He watched me and he listened to me and he walked with me and he slept with me and he knew I was ill equipped. He knew I had no place in the world, that I was at odds with it; that I was essentially alone. How this came to be, how it happened, concerned a time before his time and he didn't delve. His job, as he saw it, was damage limitation. He knew that I was temperamentally flawed, that I was without the necessary urges. I was an instinctual retreater.

It all seems so long ago now.

He once asked me what it was that I was running from; why did I choose to live amongst strangers, always on the outside of things? Why not live among your own kind? One could, he said, call it disloyal.

I agreed.

I was not as he was.

I was separate. Where this seperateness came from was never Hilly's concern. Hilly's concern was to gentle me back into the world, into a way of being that was utterly alien to me. He rode herd, he cajoled, he tempted, he wheedled, he hoped, he flattered, he begged. Oh, how he sweet talked. He brought me small gifts and left them on my pillow. He was kind and he was patient and he was determined.

He got nowhere; I was unreachable.

2

Gertrude in the morning does those things all animals do; shakes herself awake, slowly at first, then stretches, then defecates, then watches the sky, determining the upcoming weather, then places herself in the most advantageous position from which to start the day. I too do these things. In more or less the same order. When the sun is fully over the hill I turn to Gertrude and say: today let's talk about limitations.

Gertrude blows out air.

There are, I tell her, left and right, relationships and their consequences, divisions and disagreements, emulations and contentions.

Gertrude takes two steps to the left.

What Chuang Tzu called The Eight Virtues. I say.

To which Gertrude says nothing.

We spend a couple hours circling the pasture. I stick roughly at Gertrude's side. She likes me to her left, when I lag behind or drift to the right, she stomps her hooves until I assume my proper position. I watch the hovering bees; I watch Gertrude select which plant she'll eat. The day is warm but not light; there's a heaviness that seems to roll down from the hills. It's something to do with ancient mists and waters and farmers' misguided and repeated attempts to drain the fields. I've learned that Gertrude likes certain treats. I have, in my pocket, her favourite: a slice of toasted, stale bread. I give it to her and she eats it slowly, delicately. When she finishes she pushes me with her muzzle. I show her my two empty hands and she steps away.

Gertrude is a calm and dignified companion. She prefers silence but she knows humans and their weaknesses. If I feel moved to say something, so long as I keep it short and don't burst into song, she'll indulge me.

I open the gate and give her a gentle pull; she pulls back. She bends to the grass and the fresh leaves. I lean against the gate and wait.

I tell her that meliorism is the belief that the world is made better by human effort. That progress is real and quantifiable, however small, and that the engine of that progress is human endeavour.

Gertrude moves away from the gate. She turns, steps back up the slope and walks to the stable. At the stable she takes a drink. She looks at me, waggles her head and flips her tail. It seems to mean something specific. I leave the gate open and join her. We stand for a moment in the gathering sun, listening to birdsong and the stream.

Why would anyone presume that there's such a thing as progress? There are simply many and chaotic and unknowably various events. Some follow, some detract, some build, some collapse. There's no grand design, no betterment, no process. There's just stuff that happens. Where is the progress in the worldwide flood of refugees? In the mountains of discarded plastic? In the expanding number of animals and plants we daily make extinct? Where, in Syria, in Yemen, in Washington, is there progress? I watch a butterfly doing its floaty business. Gertrude snorts and gives me the big eyed stare. She makes it clear; that's enough talking for now.

3

I try and imagine how it might have been, thousands of years ago, tens of thousands, perhaps hundreds of thousands, in the time before donkeys were domesticated, when they roamed the African plains doing those things that undomesticated African donkeys did. Keeping themselves to themselves, travelling in uneven herds, eating and drinking and being mostly quiet. How they must have looked out from shaded corners and watched whatever strain of Homo sapien was then on the scene, Neanderthals or Homo Erectus, the ones who stalked ceaselessly across the desert and through the jungle. The ones with clubs and rocks. The shouty, ugly ones. The ones who chopped down that which shouldn't be chopped down, that moved that which was better left alone, that dug and stole and reordered and tinkered. The ones with ambition and big ideas. The ones without nobility, without grace. While all the while donkeys watched in quiet contemplation, patiently awaiting the day that the unsophisticated intruder, along with other ill-equipped and boorish upstarts, would disappear.

I like that the sun hits the field in the way it does. Chasing the primrose and nettles. Haloing the rosebay willowherb. All the dry stone walls ruined. Collapsed and mossy. I like not knowing who built them, whose hands thought they were necessary. The weeds at the gate are waist high. The stream falls and cuts and makes watery noise. There's a huge ash tree that sits near the house; I like the shape and weight of it. There are slate scattered paths all around. I sometimes wonder what will happen when I use up my share of time here.

People, I think, just don't know how to be lonely.

I sit here, on a bench outside my front door, eyes closed, watching Gertrude do the strangely precise things she does. Some involve eating, some involve cleaning, others involve doing nothing at all. She has a whole way of being that involves small, almost indistinguishable changes to her posture. A tilted ear, a raised hoof, a single swish of her tail. She leans forward, she hunches back, she rolls her neck. She appears unconcerned with birds and other animals smaller than herself. She sometimes, without warning, throws herself on the bare ground and thrashes around madly, hooves high. Sometimes she lays in the evening sun and snores. When I say eyes closed I mean nearly, almost – the world seen through a veil of lashes.

Beside me on the bench is my copy of Bronwyn Hanley's book. Strange companion. Each page a muttering box of intrigue, a book of exacting differences. It should never have been. How did it happen? I carry it with me on our walks and read passages to Gertrude. Today I pick a page at random, stroll over to the fence and read:
We should each of us have something beautiful to cling to. Something outside ourselves, something not grand, something unlimited. We should each try and love that thing. We should court disappointment.

Lindsay, the youngest of our tribe, has formed an alliance with Margo. He follows her day and night. His intentions are his own; with each night he grows more sure and emboldened.

There are woodpigeons cooing. They spend time behind an overgrown rose bush. The roses have fallen and the leaves are spotted. This is the time of year when things die. There is a dirt path from here that curves all the way to the sea.

Margo is indisputably beautiful, she has the tiniest ankles, the longest ears. She evokes a sense of longing. Lindsay is dark and avoids open spaces. He clings to Margo; he is changing into an older animal.

4

There are some things I think I remember.

It's not important who I am. Or, it's not important who I was. None of this is important. What, truly, is important? What and to whom? Is it important what I wear? My blouse, my shoes? The colour of my hair? The way my lips part when I speak? Whom I've married and why? What I do before I do something important? I only want to tell things plainly. I want to be precise. Precision creates a space in which to be alive. In which to be chaotic.

Do I like the silence perhaps too much? The being apart? Do I do myself a disservice by watching the shadows become less? What will it take to be different? Am I allowed to be the way I think I am? I like toast in the morning with nothing on it. I have no taste for coffee. I stopped buying butter long ago. I sit at my table and wait. This morning I lay on my cot and waited. I am a woman with no family. I am alone and yet crowded with companions. Companions of another order. Birds and mud and wood lice. These things determine the design of my life. There are, I know, entire islands in Greece where the geography is determined by donkeys. The lanes are precisely as wide as a donkey laden with grain. The distance between villages is that which can be comfortably travelled by a working donkey. The houses are built to accommodate a donkey stable. The village squares have hitching posts. The mountain roads are paved with flat rocks in deference to hooves.

Hillman operates in a world of impossibility, a world that demands more aid than can ever be given. He always used to tell me: every little bit helps.

I wonder about the constant drudgery of fixing mistakes.

The world is huge and beyond our planning. I look across damp fields agitated with life. In another hour the sun will start to fade.

Honey, I'll tell you later, says Dorothy.

Tell me now, I say.

She shakes her head and waggles a finger. I'm no imbecile, she says.

She came an hour ago, unannounced, with cheese and crackers and something in a flask. I drink tea and she drinks whatever it is she brought.

We're in the front room, one lamp on, the sky not as dark as it will be later, the moon gone then returned then gone again. Dorothy spreads out over the sofa, pushing at the room with her left hand. She has the ability to seem just a little bit more alive than everyone else.

I'll tell you this, she says.

Her left hand sweeping away.

You can talk about beauty all you want, who is and who isn't, who was and what happened, but it's all wasted breath.

She takes a swig and says, Audrey Hepburn? Ursula Andres? Coming up out of the sea in that white bikini? Beyonce? You put any of them out in these fields and birds are going to fly away, sheep will run off, fish will dive. Who really knows true beauty? We make up this shit as we go along.

Each to their own, she says.

I'm trying, in a half hearted way, to keep up.

There's only one legitimate question that anyone can ever ask anyone else.

I nod and say, what's that?

What are you doing here?

The room is silent while we think about that. Dorothy eats some cheese, I watch the bats above Gertrude's stable.

I've made some pretty good mistakes, whispers Dorothy. Lucky mistakes.

I nod. Me too, I say.

The lights from a passing truck creep slowly

across the room.

Jack The Stink's out late, says Dorothy.

He's been clearing drains, I say.

I shake my head and try not to think about Jack The Stink. A man of cheap greed and petty grievances, he owns the top fields, spraying great clouds of pesticides in the spring, poisoning badgers, terrorizing his sheep, bemoaning his poverty; roaring around in a brand new Range Rover.

Been up there all day with a tractor.

Men and their tractors, says Dorothy.

Men and their solutions. I say. Thinking of fields that once gushed and swelled with life; now a monoculture of grass. Now just sheep food. Green rugs, drained and tended and prettified. Now serving only the commerce of Man.

The night is giant, says Dorothy.

The cheese she's brought leans across the board, grey veined and soft. Hillman loved certain hard cheeses made from sheep milk. He had them for breakfast, on toast with honey. While I drank tea. He talked to several farmers about making local cheese but nothing came of it. Hillman, for all of his goodness, was no businessman.

Dorothy makes a sound as if she's been punctured.

We do get old don't we? she asks.

Yes, I say, we do.

Last night Morris got dizzy for no reason. Dizzy in the kitchen. Standing in the doorway. Stood there swaying. Saying something's wrong, something's wrong. No colour in him, washed out. Saying, I'm going to faint. I got him over to the sofa and he said, it's like I'm not here.

She expels more air.

The thing about everything is that everything gets different. No stopping anything.

I'm nibbling the edges of a cracker, the cracker has sesame seeds and black pepper on it; Dorothy is looking out at Gertrude.

Everything wearies of itself, says Dorothy.

There's a spot above my right knee that aches. I don't remember hitting or straining it. I rub the throbbing spot, pull it to me and sigh.

Remember the poetry that Morris used to write? Asks Dorothy.

Sure.

He's at it again. Bought himself a little notebook. Carries it around with him. Secretive as ever.

That's a good thing, I say.

I suppose.

She doesn't seem altogether convinced.

She purses her lips and tells me, he showed me a new one this morning.

She recites:
Our fingers
and toes
are so small
and fragile
we hide them in mittens

and socks

I watch the moon vanish. Dorothy's face falls into shadow. The room blackens. I stretch out my leg, swivel the knee and say, hellava poem. Really good.

Morris, says Dorothy, is a queer duck.

At which point I nearly laugh.

Morris is strange and always has been and is getting stranger. Says Dorothy. I'm married to a loon. One of my better mistakes.

I reach over, take Dorothy's hand and give it a squeeze.

Do we dare, I ask, go to sleep?

5

The cot is just my size. I have a blue blanket, a brown blanket, a pink one, a grey one. Also one with green and yellow stripes. A sheet too and a pillow. No light or clock. Gertrude stands ten feet away. The night is hard to know.

I'm thinking of Morris and how different he is to Hillman. In both deed and desire. And how different I am to Dorothy. And how different a bat is to a sparrow. How different each thing is to every other thing and yet how we share ears and legs and often hair. A need for water and sun. How we all swerve around doing important and less important things.

I've known Dorothy since I was born; we grew

up five miles apart. We drank the same water, shoveled the same snow, watched the same clouds that never quit; she was older and taller and seemed to have a wider range of possibilities. When I was ten she was eighteen. At twenty she married. I was so small; in October I stole apples from her parents' orchard; in March I counted lambs; in December I gathered holly. I stood for hours waiting for small things to happen. I invented a story in which every being in the world spoke a language to which I had no access; the words they spoke inhabited a different dimension; all other sounds, animal calls, rain, wind in the trees, passing trucks, were audible, but words were filtered out. I was therefore free to be silent. If I couldn't hear them I could hardly be expected to respond.

I always, though, heard Dorothy.

In those days the hills were five feet taller, the birch groves thicker, the streams wetter. There were birds then that have vanished, birds that were unable to get modern. Ground dwellers too, stoats and salamanders; animals that cleared off and disappeared.

The world we have today seems wholly new and unrelated to what went before, as if, on an April morning in 1973 the entire operation was deemed unfit for purpose, removed to some distant planet and replaced with a less delicate, less various facsimile. A pale, dumb, damp place. This new world being built of pharmaceuticals, pesticides, concrete, glamour, plastic, oil, silicone implants and fast foods. Morris told me last week that there's seven thousand tonnes of trash in space. Just floating around.

He looked at the sky and said, there's someone, right now, in a lab somewhere, California probably, figuring out how to breed robot space monkeys in order to clean everything up.

His fields and mine, this upland corner, though lessened by us, is not so damaged as most. We live outside the worst.

When I was younger and less sure of who I was, before I met Hillman, before The Sewing Basket, before most of my life, I tried to be another kind of person and failed. I denied who I was and spent some time falling apart; at my lowest point Dorothy and Morris took me in; I lived with them for six months. I spent my afternoons doing small, specific chores over which I took elaborate care. Dorothy let me be quiet and Morris treated me as he treated all the other animals; he told me strange facts and rubbed my head and made sure I had enough to eat. The days had an erratic routine. Jobs were done in the order in which they were discovered. Fences mended, potholes filled, animals doctored, wood cut. There was no plan, no strategy. In the morning Morris walked around the place saying, que faites-vous tous ici? The house, the fields, the barns and gardens, all was in a state of revision. Slowly I was made less messy but still wary.

With Dorothy in the evenings I shared something called SleepEZE tea. It came in a bright box that featured pictures of sleeping animals, dogs and cats and birds and bugs and tigers and rabbits. We drank it while we whispered about the day. Morris went into the bedroom and looked after himself. Dorothy told me that there was no great difference between desire and hope and hate and affection but that people read books that said there was and so they believed it. She said that what most people do is they spend their lives maintaining differences that don't exist. She often went to sleep there on the sofa, sitting beside me, her hand on my shoulder. There was always so much to do, feeding animals and gardening and pruning and clearing and moving things from place to place. Dorothy said that if life is all confusion and failure and small winnings then the best way to get through it was not to try and tidy things up too much. Let it be all curious and wanton.

Suze, she once said, I've seen more than my fair share of energetic goings on.

The chamomile steam from her SleepEZE tea clung to her hair. It smelled of honey and lemon and vanilla too. She leaned against me and said, we must not be too sad in this sorrowful place.

6

Just before dawn Gertrude brays twice. Then once. Then twice more. Then a whole string of them. She's stomping around over there and kicking and her ears are laid back. At first I think she's asleep and dreaming and then I think maybe she was at first but now she's awake and scared and I don't know why. I lay here for a moment and then go to her. I stroke her head and haunches and whisper that everything's OK. I quiet her down and look around the stable. I see nothing out of the ordinary. I can feel her heart racing. She pushes her head against my chest and I blow air into her ears. She exhales loudly and snorts. I rub her nose. We stand together and after a while the sun is barely there behind the bracken, rising over the hill, the light limp and without heat. There are birds as well, doing what birds do; the hill pales. Slowly Gertrude calms and regains her usual sense of composure.

Hey girl, I whisper, what was that all about?

When it's fully light we take up our usual position near the fence. I'm giving Gertrude a brush when I hear a car come grumbling up the lane. It's not a car I've seen before. Something new, perhaps rented, without dents or mud. It slows as it approaches the house, stopping just in front of Gertrude and myself. The only occupant of the car, an elderly man, leans out his window and asks if I live here.

I try, I say.

Do you succeed?

Occasionally.

He smiles at that and turns off the engine.

I know this place, he says.

Do you?

He opens his door, steps outside and leans against the car. Neither of us say anything. He looks like someone's grandfather. He's staring back up the road; he squints and shakes his head.

We used to come out here, he says. Me and my wife. Sit here in our car and drink tea.

Gertrude's mane has become softer. Something to do with losing her winter coat. Last week I bought shears and gave her a haircut. I nod at the man.

There used to be a caravan, he says. Over there. Beneath that ash tree.

Was there?

Little metal box. Forty years ago. Never saw anyone in it.

I look at his spotted hands, his yellow nails. He looks at my house and asks, how long you been here?

All my life, I say. I moved here ten years ago.

You like it?

I move my shoulders. I try to, I say.

It'd be an easy place to like, he says.

I want to tell him that nothing's easy for me. I want to say that like it or hate it, it's where I live and that means something big. It means that I'm here and I have to deal with the problems that being here brings. I put down Gertrude's comb on a fence post. The sun is directly overhead. Gertrude noses the comb and gives me a hurt look.

We lived in the mid-lands then, says the man.

He's not happy saying the words *mid-lands*. It's not a phrase he enjoys.

Used to drive over here and play games.

Games?

Where we'd live if we had the choice. What we'd do if we were different kinds of people. What kind of house we'd have. What-ifs and maybes. Animals, kids, trees, garden. Just sit here talking nonsense.

I nod.

You live here alone?

I point at Gertrude and say, just the two of us.

He looks back down the lane and says, thirty years.

Gertrude loses interest and turns away, looking for something to graze.

I wondered if it was still here, he says.

It's all different, I tell him.

Is it? Feels just the same to me. With the exception of the caravan it's exactly as I remember it.

I watch the light get hung up in the trees.

We used to park next to it, he says. The caravan. On the weekends. In our Capri. Ford Capri.

His hands are splattered with dark spots. He rubs one across the roof and says, never saw a soul. No one.

You can still do that, I say. Sit here all day and not see anyone.

People, he says.

People, I say.

It doesn't seem like he needs to talk too much. Mostly he just wants to stand around and not be where he was this morning. He squints into the sun and says, fine looking donkey.

Yes she is.

Went once to..., What was it called?

He does something with his right hand.

Hydra. Greek island. You ever?

I shake my head. Gertrude looks up and snorts.

Donkeys everywhere.

His hair, what's left of it, is white. He keeps it short. He wears, on his left wrist, a single gold chain.

I live in Amsterdam now, he says. Just outside. Fifteen years.

He looks at me and says, you ever?

I don't travel, I tell him.

Pretty place. Flat. Good people.

He lets a minute go by and says, Caroline used to complain about where we were living and what the street looked like. The smell of the gas works. Litter and fly tipping and all that. She'd tell me I should quit my job and we should come out here and get rural. Find ourselves somewhere exactly like this.

It's not for everyone, I say.

Gertrude comes over and gives my shoulder a nudge.

Suits her, I say, stroking her nose.

He laughs and says, I guess it would. Free room and board, get your hair combed and your hooves trimmed, hang around all day doing nothing. No taxes, no neighbours, no police.

He says that last sentence as if he's practiced saying it. Taxes, neighbours, police. As if he's not yet forgiven something. Two magpies come rattling down from the trees, squawking, tumbling onto the road.

You work? He asks me.

Everybody works.

He nods and I say, in town. In a shop.

You like it?

I don't hate it.

Fair enough.

He scratches at the back of his neck and says, smells different here. Than home. Where I live.

He pokes out his nose and sniffs.

Holland has a flatter smell. Smells like hills here.

Neither of us have anything to say to that. We stand in the yellow light and listen to those things hill people listen to; birds and bugs and wind in the leaves and tractors a mile away. Finally he pushes away from the car, grunts and says, well.

I'm wondering if maybe there's something he wants before his drive back, a cup of tea or water, and he says, you mind if I sit here a for minute and have a drink?

He points to a flask sitting on the passenger's seat.

I got some coffee, he says.

Of course. You're welcome to...

I point out the bench that came with the house, where I spend my mornings, in the shade of an ash tree. We go over there and sit for a minute and I wonder if he wants to be left alone. I'm thinking: he hasn't driven all this way to sit and talk to me. Just as I'm about to get up he takes a big breath and starts telling me about Caroline and her sister and how they all shared a house together in Wolverhampton and about the job he had selling patio furniture and how much he hated it and how everything went wrong the year Caroline died and he ended up asking the sister to marry him but the sister said no and moved to Devon and then he started drinking and lost his job and he fell in with some people that were best avoided and did some things of which he wasn't proud and ended up in jail for a year and when he got out he went to Holland and liked it and managed to get a job there and stay.

What I do now, he says, is I work in a warehouse. Sending flowers around the world. Tulips and orchids.

He's talking the way people talk when they're talking to someone they'll never see again. He screws the lid on his flask and makes one of those airy noises old men make. Caroline, he says, always had problems with her lungs. Asthma, bronchitis, that sort of show. She said she could breathe better out here.

He looks at me and asks, whatta you think? You breathe better out here?

Maybe, I say.

I nod at the pasture and say, Gertrude seems to breathe pretty good.

Gertrude is slowly circling the field, watching, grazing, resting, breathing.

Caroline left me once, he says. Went to Hull.

Gertrude, on the far side of the pasture, lets out a low nicker. Three black birds sit on the telephone wire. A dog, across the valley, barks.

Where Philip Larkin lived. You ever?

Left someone or gone to Hull?

Both.

Yes and no. Yes to leaving, no to Hull.

Ever read him? Larkin?

I nod and he says, Caroline was doing a further education thing. Evening classes. Poetry and that.

He tells the rest of it and he tells it quickly and it takes a while. About how Caroline went to Hull and what she did there and how, eventually, they got back together and then how she died. When he's finished he leans back and rubs his hand across his face. Gertrude is nearly back to the gate. The sun is approaching the top of the chestnut tree. I'm hungry enough to notice I'm hungry. I don't know what to say. When have I ever known what to say? I sit and say nothing. Finally he stands.

She was stubborn, he says.

I nod.

She loved it here.

Another nod.

And –

His hand arcs across the yard.

I've got a long drive ahead of me.

He looks east, as if looking across the country. Were you married? he asks.

Sometimes.

Was it good?

Sometimes.

There's a sound that comes skittling through the aspens and pushing at the bracken. A smell too of things damp and hidden and gone soft. We sit for a moment; his trousers are a thin blueish grey, of the kind worn by men who are unaccustomed to leisure. He smells, slightly, of soap.

Do you know a poem Larkin wrote entitled Home Is So Sad?

I nod and say, yes.

He begins to say something but stops. He sucks in air through his teeth. He wears neither watch nor ring. His time here is finished. He stands, slowly unfolding each part of his body, knees, hips, chest, neck. He reaches down and retrieves his flask. We walk to his car. Gertrude, at the gate, raises her head as we pass.

I look at her guiltily; our afternoon walk untaken. I make a silent promise to walk twice as far tomorrow.

In his car he settles behind the wheel and buckles his seat belt. He takes his time. He glances once in the rear view mirror and releases the hand brake. His eyes are clear. He turns the key, leans out the window and points a flattened hand at me. The hand, as he drives away, does a little wavy type thing.

7

Nothing happens again and again. It never stops. There are evenings and mornings and half-lit Sundays. We are permanently unhomed. We pretend and are unsuited for pretence; we are each aged differently. The skies are all white. I once told Hillman that I couldn't bear to hear him talk the way he talked. Not for another minute. After he had told me that we each must be our own angels. That we must be confident in our doing. That we mustn't lose track of how things get better. That we must do good because that's what God wants us to do.

One person believes things unimaginable to the next.

I told him that we lie to ourselves because we must.

SEPTEMBER

She stands in the black spotted shade of a syca-more; at her feet are two saplings. On the trunk of the tree is a bird box. Empty now. The ground is scattered with leaves; the leaves will continue to fall all winter. The day is cool and getting cold. A rain that doesn't fall, that hangs in the air, that's all over murky, has turned things dank.

She watches the swallows leave their nests in search of insects, sees them swoop and dive above the house, readying themselves. Soon they'll leave their nests altogether, in route to other, better lit places, other continents, other nests, other airborne bugs.

How long before the first snow? A month? Two months? Or, like last year, will it not snow at all, but just go cold and dark and be always wet? The fields pooled and puddled. The mud without precedent. She walks across the yard toward the gate, to the pasture, to Gertrude, in her wool jumper and thick socks, her hat with a bauble on top.

Gertrude has, in preparation for the winter, put on a few pounds. Her coat is thicker. She stands patiently by the gate.

In eight months the swallows will return from Africa, from warmth, from uncountable distances, to fall and circle above the house. To be quick, dark marks against the sky. While she, beneath the same sycamore, saying nothing, will watch on.

Suzanne walks on ahead while Gertrude considers a clump of weeds. There is, somewhere above, a sun; the graveled lane is bordered by hedgerows. Suzanne looks back over her shoulder and says, guess what I've got.

She reaches into her pocket and pulls out an apple. She holds it up and Gertrude steps quickly forward. The apple, a small Cox, disappears in one delicate bite, leaving, on Suzanne's palm, a smear of saliva. The sky and all it contains grows lighter, the greyness is briefly tinged with yellow. Suzanne rubs Gertrude's ears and thinks of the lake they've just left and how it was once surrounded by marshlands. It was a favourite place to come with Hillman; they'd pick their way through the boggy fields, find a dry corner, and, amongst the water voles and yellow irises, have a picnic of stale bread and hard cheese. Now grass grows to the waters edge. The fields have been drained and sprayed in order to provide more sheep grazing. The world and all its resources have been put to work; those creatures not of immediate benefit are expendable.

As they walk home the fog thickens; the silence is utter, the air furred, they can see no further than the hedged walls. Gertrude, unwilling to be parted from Suzanne, keeps her head near Suzanne's waist. Suzanne makes little sounds to comfort Gertrude. C'mon girl, she says. Nearly home.

In the late evening she sits on the sofa and eats a sandwich. Beside her is an opened book. A section of text has been marked with a pencil:
Allow the process of change to go unimpeded, and learn to grow old. Plunge into the unknown and the endless and find your place there.
Do not hanker for fame.
Do not make plans.
Do not try and do things.
Do not try and master knowledge.
Hold what is but do not hold it to be anything.
Just be empty.
In front of her the TV flickers. A man and woman are sitting in a glamorous, riverside restaurant. Through one of the windows we see the Eiffel tower. Champagne is ordered. All around the room beautiful people sit beautifully. The couple chat, waiters stand by, the music swells. The scene cuts to three men in ski masks entering the kitchen. They each pull out guns and start shooting. There are slow motion shots of bullets flying, glass shattering, cooks falling, arcs of blood mixing with broth. The killers run from the kitchen into the dining area and threaten the crowd. It's clear they're looking for the man who was sitting with the woman. The man,

however, is gone. The woman cowers beneath the table. The killers approach her and pull her to her feet. At that moment, through the window, we see the man in a speed boat, escaping into the night.

Suzanne sighs and turns off the TV. She looks out the window and can see only fog. She puts down her plate and whispers, water, hay, blanket, gate. She closes the book; on its cover are the words *Less Than This – The Writings Of Chuang Tzu.* The wood stove crackles as she whispers, water, hay, blanket, gate. She takes her plate and cup into the kitchen. Standing at the sink she whispers again, water, hay, blanket, gate. Before she goes to bed she'll go out and check on Gertrude. A nightly ritual. Water, hay, blanket, gate.

2

```
Suzanne Welch
Ty Nant
Llanisflyn
Wales
SY 21 9HK

Suzanne —

I was, yesterday, forcefully removed
from Douma. For my own good, they tell
me. We have a strict policy: two weeks
on, two days off. We're told to look
after ourselves so that we can look
after others. I was brought here to
```

this tent and told to sleep. As if, in this heat, that's an option. Who sleeps in Syria? The noise is constant; the shelling, the jets, the helicopters, the gun fire; the death rattle of the locals.

I remind myself that I at least have a bed, I have water, I have food, I have the possibility of escape.

I have the memory of you and Ty Nant and the knowledge that, if needs be, I can return there.

Ten days ago someone, who knows, Assad or Putin or some enterprising, impatient underling, dropped chemical bombs on the eastern section of the city. Bombs containing military grade ammonia. Our aid station was five miles away. We spent 48 hours pouring water over the burning heads of children. There was nothing else to do — we rounded up those who survived, doused them, and got them to the clearing house that passes for a field hospital.

This, these past three months, doesn't much feel like aid work. To whom am I giving aid? More die than can be helped. We step over dead bodies to get to wounded bodies that die on the way to the hospital.

Yesterday I sat for three hours holding the hand of a girl whose entire family had been killed. And when I say holding her hand I mean the left hand because the right hand was gone, blown off a couple months ago.

The director tells me that there used to be packs of scavengers, cats and dogs and rats and mice, that followed the aid trucks, but now there's nothing. No animals, no plants, nothing. Only dust. And watch out, the director said, the dust is toxic. Stay indoors as much as possible. The dust will strip your throat and ruin your lungs.

We do what we can.

Sorrow, yes. Blood, yes. Slaughter and havoc, yes. All here, on our doorstep. I know it used to upset you when I tried to tell you why I do what I do. God Talk, you called it. Perhaps it was. Perhaps that was the way I understood it. Now, I'm not so sure. Now I think I'm here because I'm the sort of person that ends up here. It's who I am. I'm a type. I recognize others of my tribe. We barely bother with names.

The director and I share a tent. She calls me Number Four. She quotes Primo Levi at me: We all know perfect happiness is impossible, fewer of us realize that perfect unhappiness is also impossible. She came here from the camps in Yemen. The war drove them out. Something happened there, something she won't talk about, something to do with government sanctioned pirates; a fight or an ambush or a dropped crate; she walks with a limp. She snakes around the place making sure everything is working as best it can. The best it can isn't very good. We're under staffed and under supported and too much is expected of us. We're hated and we're worshipped. We do what we do because we're the kind of people who can't do anything else.

We have two major reasons for being here: medical supplies and food. That's what it all boils down to. Drugs and rice. We're supposed to keep strict records of what we have but it's impossible. Supplies go missing every day. They walk out the front door, they melt into the air, they fade into the sand. They're traded for protection, used as bargaining chips, consumed by friendly fire. We do what we can. We pick our battles.

The director told me, when I arrived here this morning, to forget the weekly inventory. We'll have to get around it, she said. Somehow. Be creative. She said she'd given 300 lbs of rice to a warlord in exchange for six kidnapped children. No questions asked. A gesture of good faith. Good faith to a man who has personally ordered the burning of entire villages. She handed over the rice and the children were delivered an hour later. Each one worth 50 lbs of rice.

The director limps in and hovers.

I'm fine, I tell her. I hold up this
letter and say, I'm writing home. Home,
she mumbles, as if unfamiliar with
the concept. Not giving away secrets
are you? she asks. She's American, a
former academic, a Quaker; she has, on
the table next to her bed, a framed
picture of Dorothy Day. Her only words
of advice, on the day I arrived, were,
do what you think best and do it
quickly. Let God sort out the details.
She's been here five years, before
that in Yemen, before that Palestine.
She's learned to be unsettled. She's
forgotten how to sleep; she sends me
whispers from across the room. She told
me, one night, that God didn't intend
that there be war and poverty and
persecution of one man by another. All
this constant disastering, she said,
is our making not his. And as it's the
way we've organized it and it's us that
maintain it, it's up to us to change
it.

She tells me snippets of her life
before she left America. There was, I
gather, a relationship with a fellow
academic, a woman, that ended badly.

Sometimes, she whispers, things go
well until they go wrong and then they
go away and don't come back.

I tell her about you and Ty Nant
and Wales and how we lived there and
why I left. Except that I don't know,
exactly, why I left.

I know very little, exactly.

I know a great deal, vaguely.

I know that in Japan, a thousand years ago, when they built the great gardens at Kyoto, they placed the paving stones at slightly irregular intervals, so that anyone walking too fast would stumble. They wanted people to slow down, to take a look around. I know that I'll be here for a while. I know that what we do is we go on.

Until we don't.

Tell Gertrude and Dorothy that I send what little love I can manage.

I save most of it for you.

Yours,

H

3

In the morning Suzanne stands with Gertrude and watches three black birds in a bare oak tree. All the field is wilted. Suzanne wears boots, a denim jacket, jeans, three shirts, a hat and gloves. Gertrude wears her blanket. Suzanne pulls her fingers through Gertrude's mane and says, there are places in the world different to this one.

The black birds fly away and are replaced by three magpies.

Did you know that?

Gertrude leans into Suzanne's hands. The magpies hop from limb to limb.

There are tall places that have been flattened and flat places that have been rubbled. Places gassed and oiled.

She kneads the muscles at the base of Gertrude's neck.

Places where bugs and beetles and lice and spiders have been finished.

Gertrude snorts and stamps.

All because someone, somewhere, first got greedy and then got greedier. Says Suzanne.

Dorothy slams the car door and waves. Suzanne, by the gate, nods.

Surprise, says Dorothy. Morris had to go to town, pick up something for the tractor. Left me to amuse myself.

Suzanne steps forward and they embrace. The wind blows on them.

So I, asks Suzanne, I'm your amusement?

Something like that, says Dorothy.

They look across the yard at Gertrude. She stands next to her stable, tail flickering, giving them the big eyed stare.

Big eyed stare, says Suzanne.

The wind is low, knee high, running close to the ground, bothering mice and gorse. Suzanne tugs at her jeans and leads the way to the front door. On the door is a knocker in the shape of a woodpecker.

What we'll talk about today, says Dorothy, are

local characters and how they got so dull.

They sit near the window so they can see the world. The world is older than both of them put together but the autumn cold is new. They sit side by side with their hips and shoulders touching. Dorothy's hair is bouncing all over the place.

Washed it this morning with something green that involved seaweed, says Dorothy. And now it's done this.

She came with it stuffed into a knit cap; now it's afroing around her face. Suzanne smiles and pokes at it with her finger.

Winnie The Church, says Dorothy, called me last night. Asked me to join her book club.

She manages to look both horrified and bored at the same time.

A club! Says Dorothy. Where you read books! I told her that reading isn't a team sport. I said I had no interest in discussing the books I read with anyone else. Reading is a solo pursuit, like gardening and showering, and that, I'm afraid, is that.

Suzanne nods and says, Eve The Library is always trying to interest me in audio books.

Dorothy grimaces and says, since when can we not make time to sit down and be alone with a book? Why involve another school of technology? You might as well watch a movie or TV. The text becomes the property of a third party. Means you're no longer alone. Also means you can do two things at once. Which, frankly, is a wrong thing. Which, frankly, means doing two things badly. If you can listen to a book and at the same time cook or knit or drive or paint, then either the book isn't worth listening to or you're listening badly. Either way, stop it!

Suzanne laughs and Dorothy leans. The afternoon sky is not friendly. What I mean isn't easy, says Dorothy.

Suzanne nods and says, this specific time, this time we're in now, is wearying.

Sure it is. Says Dorothy.

There's only a few like us around. Says Suzanne.

She says this in a way that shows she's not bragging or pleased or wishful.

That's a fact. Says Dorothy.

The fact, says Suzanne, is that I'm tired.

Tired?

Suzanne swings her head close to Dorothy's shoulder. The sleeve of Dorothy's shirt is faded blue. Suzanne can feel, beneath the thin cotton, hard muscle. They sit silently for one, two, three minutes.

I found a poem last night, says Dorothy. One of Morris's. On the barn floor. Written on the back of a sales receipt. Must have fallen out of his jacket.

Suzanne waits.

I've got it here.

Dorothy twists around, reaches over and pulls it from her bag. She hands it to Suzanne.

The plate

and cup
and spoon
are set.
They wait
while I
add pepper
to the beans.

Suzanne smiles and hands it back to Dorothy.

Morris doesn't make much sense, says Dorothy, to anyone but Morris.

Suzanne nods, brushing her chin against Dorothy's shirt. There is, on the wall near the window, a small painting of a red dog.

I think Gertrude, says Suzanne, is the same.

The same as Morris?

In the not making sense way. To anyone but herself.

The red dog, a terrier, is laying on a green lawn. It has a yellow ribbon around its neck.

I think I've changed, says Suzanne. I feel just like a Deborah. Or a Patricia maybe. Or an Isabel. Someone not like me anymore.

Dorothy slips her hand over Suzanne's and says, I once temporarily lost my vigor and when it came back it was all different, a different potency, but I recognized it as mine and it took a minute to get used to it, to my new vigor, the new feel of it, but eventually I did and here I am, restored.

She squeezes Suzanne's hand and says, we've both lived for years.

Suzanne nods and looks at the red dog, the green lawn, the yellow ribbon.

Gertrude, she says, behaves properly and isn't gloomy and stands just right amongst the dead grass.

She says this knowing it to be true.

4

Night falls early. The world is without. Fewer hours of light, fewer birds, fewer flowers, fewer leaves. Sounds too are less, the evening is muffled. Gertrude crowds the stable door. Suzanne approaches holding out an empty hand. In her other hand is a small yellow apple. They stand for a moment pushing at each other; Suzanne gives up the apple and Gertrude happily chews.

The clouds are fewer too, which means the stars can be seen. Suzanne looks south across the hills. The stars don't sparkle. Neither do they dance. They shine dully. Suzanne looks straight up, into the web of lights.

Somewhere up there, she tells Gertrude, are two constellations named for you. The Northern Donkey and The Southern Donkey. Asellus Boralis and Asellus Australis. I don't know where they are or what they look like or who named them or why they were named after donkeys. Morris told me about them.

She strokes Gertrude's back and says, Morris

knows everything.

And nothing.

He told me that Dionysus and his friend, the god of fire, were riding their donkeys into battle against an army of giants and the donkeys began braying and the giants, who had never heard such a sound before, thought a terrible monster was coming and ran away. Pathetic giants. Morris said that Dionysus was rarely without his donkey. Which I think speaks well of Dionysus, don't you?

She rubs Gertrude's ears and Gertrude sighs.

Dionysus, she says, being the Greek god of wine and merriment.

The stars, briefly, are shrouded. They blink off and then, in a moment, return.

Wine and merriment being in short supply around these parts.

She can see, near the quarry, a sliver of moon. The cold is hardening the air. Several large birds drift in the darkness.

She shakes her head and says, or perhaps it's the opposite. Depending on the company you keep.

She rests against Gertrude.

What do you think? Too much or not enough?

Gertrude says nothing.

5

Suzanne in The Sewing Basket unpacks a shipment of cotton reels. The box in which they came has split and the reels are jumbled together; she's sorting them according to size and colour. The day has been mostly slow. There was a rush around noon but all afternoon it's been empty. When the bell rings she looks up. A woman is squinting into the room. She has about her the look of dislocation. Not a local. Suzanne adds a green reel to the pile and asks, can I help you?

I'm looking, the woman says, for Suzanne Welch.

For a moment Suzanne considers lying. This can't be good. What good has ever come from a stranger asking questions?

She picks up a yellow reel and says, that's me.

The woman steps into the room and looks around the shop. I've come, she says, from Manchester. On the train.

Suzanne nods.

The woman steps to the counter and extends her hand.

Meredith. Meredith Samuels.

Suzanne shakes her hand.

She's not, Suzanne thinks, selling anything. The fabric reps and salesmen come the first week of the month, stinking of cheap coffee and breath freshener, carrying huge sample bags.

I was hoping, the woman says, to catch you as you were closing.

You've done it. Just tidying up some loose ends.

Is there somewhere we could talk? Alone?

Suzanne crosses the room and flips the Open sign to Closed. She turns off the main lights.

We can talk here.

Suzanne returns to the counter and pulls out a second chair. They both sit. The woman unbuttons her coat and, from an inside pocket, pulls out a business card.

We don't have a phone number for you on file, she says. And anyway, I thought it best I come in person.

She hands Suzanne the card. The card says Meredith Samuels – Foreign Office – Overseas Aid and Development.

What's this about?

I'm afraid, says Meredith Samuels, that I have bad news.

Bad news?

Your husband, says Meredith Samuels.

Hillman?

Yes.

I'm not sure how to tell you this.

Suzanne looks at the pulsing vein in Ms. Samuels neck and knows, suddenly, exactly why she's come. The knowledge hammers her. The room is emptied. Her knees, her shoulders, her feet, her head; she reels back and hears nothing.

Long after Ms. Samuels has left Suzanne sits in the shop. She finishes sorting the cotton reels, tidies the day's receipts and turns off the light. There's air all around her. She sits with her hands in her lap, her eyes closed. The town is trying to be quiet. A few cars, a dog, a church bell. The hushed rattle of a train.

It was, Ms. Samuels had said, bad luck. In the wrong place at the wrong time.

And Suzanne had wondered, is death bad luck? Surely it's being born that's bad luck. And aren't all of us, you and me both, perpetually in the wrong place at the wrong time?

He was delivering aid to a hospital when a landmine went off. He was killed instantly; two others survived for a few hours.

It was awful, a dreadful waste, Ms. Samuels had said.

And Suzanne had thought, it's all awful, all a dreadful waste. All of it. Every inch and ounce of it. All this breathing and wishing and being and doing.

I'm just so, so sorry. Said Ms. Samuels.

Suzanne sits as a woman in a painting sits. Hands folded, eyes down. In shadows. A cat, on her lap, she thinks, would be a comfort. Or a dog. A breathing thing not given to speech. The dusk burrows into her; like a rabbit, like a mole, like a rat. She thinks: maybe everything that's ever going to happen in my life has happened. She's both under and over whelmed. It's as if she's feeling in a foreign language; having to translate her own emotions. The area between her arms, between her breasts and her shoulder blades, is large and wide and unlit; dry somehow and flat.

Hillman is dead.

The light in the room is stolen from the street. She tips forward and stands, one hand on the counter. She feels as if she's carrying a random weight, all of her forever unbalanced. One foot thick, the other made of paper. She tells herself: go home. Now. You can do this. Step across the room, open the door, walk down Market Street, past the library, past the market hall. Past the bank. Get in your car and drive home. Do it now and be there.

Be at home with Gertrude.

Now.

6

They went away because they were tired. That's what they told each other – we're tired and need a rest. Tired of what and for what reasons were conversations they saved for later. They decided on the coast. They took a box of food, a tent and some bedding; they headed north and west. They drove through Harlech, Porthmadog, Criccieth, Pwllheli. By late afternoon, having reached the end of the road, they found an empty corner and pitched a tent. They were just outside of Aberdaron. The ocean rolled before them; unknowable and huge and filled with those things which are least explainable. They sat and watched. The salted wind pushed at them. There were bugs and swallows in the dusk. Also the sound of gulls and the constant spray of the waves. Also, behind them, fields of grey sheep.

They laid back on the grass and stared at the sky. Many things and nothing were happening up there. Some of it was purpled, other places were pink; it spread out immensely, from Lagos to Paris. Hillman placed his hand on Suzanne's leg, fingering her knee.

They talked about the health of an elderly farmer who lived a mile from them; he'd fallen, cut his leg, and neglected to go to the doctor. The cut became infected and now he was in bed with blood poisoning.

I'll stop in and see him when we get back, Suzanne had said. See if he needs anything.

In two weeks he would be dead, his body too old and weak to fight the poison. His land and livestock would be sold at auction; his tractor and machinery left to rust, his house abandoned.

Did you know, Hillman had asked, that when we're born we have three hundred bones in our body and at the end of our lives, when we die, we have two hundred and six?

How does that work?

Hillman made a sound that resembled satin rustling.

They calcify, he said.

Suzanne had rotated her left shoulder and

nodded. An airplane was working its way slowly out towards Ireland.

They join together, said Hillman. They merge.

So what you're saying is…

I'm saying that we get more dense. We stiffen.

You're telling me we fossilize, said Suzanne.

We harden. Yes.

They spoke quietly then of the world; wars of all kinds, economic and otherwise, man-made plagues, holocausts, the enrichment and pleasuring of the rich, disasters on all fronts. The airplane disappeared and was replaced by another. The sky was less purple, less pink, more grey. A boat's horn sounded. Gulls bawled. Behind them the sheep retreated against a stone wall.

A month later Hillman left.

7

Gertrude stands patiently by the stable. Suzanne, her arms full of blankets and pillows and candles and sheets, crosses the field. She reaches the stable and drops everything on the cot. Gertrude lets out a half whinny, half sneeze. The night is crowded with stars and bats and nocturnal doings. It's cold but not unpleasantly so. Leaves drift around the door. Suzanne puts her arm around Gertrude's neck and says, I'm going to move back in for a few days.

Gertrude stomps her hoof a couple of times and says nothing.

Suzanne doesn't sleep. Sleep is an inaccessible, empty field. She stands, locked out, at the gate. She watches the dark outline of Gertrude and listens to her breathing. The smell of her is everywhere; the smell of soil and time and weather and being solitary. She pulls the blankets up over her chin.

There is, she thinks, too much.

It hunkers on her, the weightiness of living. She makes out Gertrude's tail in the darkness, swinging left to right, flickering. She remembers something she once read by Wordsworth: there had passed away a glory from the earth.

She huddles down into her blankets. There's an owl out there doing its hooty thing. Another owl answers. It goes back and forth, back and forth. She turns on her side and pushes back hair from her eyes. Her lips are dry, her teeth ache. The pain, above her right knee, has returned.

At dawn, she's awoken by a scream. A yelping terror. The sound comes knifing through the night. She sits up and waits while her eyes adjust. Gertrude is still in the stable, pressed against the wall. The scream comes again, slightly quieter this time. Suzanne stands, crosses the stable and strokes Gertrude's mane. What is that? she asks.

Gertrude shuffles and turns towards the door. They each step into the morning.

Streaks of light stripe the field. Trees, lit from

below, lean over dried clumps of bracken. Blown leaves cling to the fence. Molehills dot the slope.

And again, the whimpering yelp.

Suzanne and Gertrude walk slowly up the hill, away from the stable, in the direction of the noise. Gertrude's hooves and Suzanne's boots, in the morning dew, are quickly soaked. Suzanne pushes on ahead; c'mon slow coach, she says.

They reach the ridge and stand for a moment, uncertain of where to turn. Above them, in a syca-more, three blackbirds do what morning birds do. The light grows stronger.

They hear it again, across the fields and over by the quarry, coming from somewhere inside Jack The Stink's land. A sound of distress. C'mon, says Suzanne.

They follow the ridge until they come to a gate. Suzanne opens it and they step onto a bridleway. In a hundred yards they come to another gate where they enter Jack The Stink's pastures. The sound comes again, fainter, from near a stand of alders.

Gertrude is in no hurry. She stops at every clump of grass. Her ears twist, her tail swings. She refuses to go forward. Suzanne beckons and begs and finally gives up. She goes on ahead and when she reaches the alders she hears a low groan-ing. The trees give no shelter, the sky is uncertain. She walks carefully between them, watching the ground, and in the middle of the stand she finds it. A fox in a trap. The animal is covered in blood and seems unaware of her presence. It's left hip has been smashed, gripped between the jaws of the trap. Its eyes are glazed with terror; its mouth hangs open. The ground around it is blood soaked; its breathing is irregular; the air is heavy with musk.

As Suzanne bends to it, it summons what small reserves of strength it has left and snarls. Its teeth, bared, are blood-covered.

Now, now, she says.

She steps back, takes off her coat and kneels. Making a sound she imagines to be comforting she drops the coat on the fox. She hears it thrash once and go silent. Its breathing is increasingly erratic. She looks for and finds the release lever at the back of the trap, presses it, and the jaws spring open. With one hand she holds the fox still, with the other she slides the trap away. The teeth of the trap are clotted with blood, flesh and hair. She bends forward and pulls the coat and fox to her. The fox, beneath the blue wool jacket, is too weak to resist. Suzanne cradles it into her lap and slowly strokes its back.

I'm sorry, she whispers.

I'm sorry.

After a moment she looks up to see Gertrude standing six feet away. Gertrude looks at her, blows out air, sneezes, and bends to the grass.

Suzanne can feel the last flutters of life in the fox. Her eyes fill with tears; she blinks them away.

I'm sorry. She says.

The sun is higher now, above the bare oaks. The day is not cold, not wet, not grey, not bright. A thin fog has crept down from the hills and now sits close to the ground. It won't last. In another hour the day will be as September days often are, distinctly edged and brittle. The day will promise nothing, hide nothing, deliver little, provide no comfort.

The fox is limp. It hangs across Suzanne's lap. What was alive is now dead. She closes her eyes and takes a deep breath. After a moment she removes the coat. The fox is still a fox. Mangled and tortured and made dead, but still a fox. Perhaps the same fox that once circled Ty Nant. Perhaps the same fox that left pheasant feathers at her gate.

She stands, carrying the fox. It weighs little, less that a bolt of fabric. She walks deeper into the alders until she finds a rocky out cropping. The rock is smooth and wind rubbed, covered in greenish moss and lichen. At the base of the rock is a circle of dead bracken. She places the fox in the center of the circle and says, I'm sorry.

She hears Gertrude snorting.

The fox lays twisted and misshapen, a lump of skin and tongue and tail and nose. She can think of nothing to say. She returns to her coat and finds Gertrude waiting. She pats Gertrude's head and Gertrude brays.

Yes, yes, says Suzanne.

The fog is already clearing. Uneven light floats

across the field. Two rooks and a pheasant skitter through the fence. She looks down at the rusty trap, picks up a stone and drops it; the trap snaps in two. She pats Gertrude on her haunches and says, c'mon girl.

She picks up the soiled coat and puts it on. It has a large indeterminately shaped stain on the back. Dead leaves and twigs cling to it. A cuff, where it lay under the fox, has been made brown.

In this way, with the coat wrapped around her, smelling of fear and outrage and torment and urine, they head slowly for home.

8

In the morning Suzanne drives to town and leaves a note on the door of The Sewing Basket.

DUE TO AN UNFORESEEN DEATH
WE WILL BE CLOSED FOR ONE WEEK.

On the drive home she wonders if the death refers to Hillman or the fox. She had awoken, that morning, feeling unrested and suspicious. She suspects that she may have spent the night dreaming. She remembers nothing. She worries that she's turning into a different kind of person. She wonders if the death of a loved one allows you to live in a way that you wouldn't ordinarily live.

The wind is up, plastic bags and leaves jump across the road. The fields feel even more empty than is usual. She passes no other cars. She drives slowly, alert to disaster.

When she gets home she calls Dorothy and tells her about Hillman. After a moment's silence Dorothy sighs and says, damn.

Yea. Says Suzanne.

Damn.

The phone makes the distance between them feel much further than it is. Five miles feels like five hundred. The silence is not silent.

You there?

Yea. Says Suzanne. I guess so. Barely.

I'll come over.

Suzanne nods and says, I don't want to talk about it.

Fine. You don't have to. We'll sit.

OK. Thanks.

Suzanne watches a robin on the gate post. Orange and brown and grey and black. It puffs out its chest, raises its beak and is noisy.

I'll be in the stable.

They will each take up space in the stabled gloom. Suzanne and Dorothy on the cot, Gertrude against the wall, Dorothy with a flask, Suzanne with a mug. The thing is, Dorothy will say.

Suzanne will lean forward, anxious to hear the thing.

The thing is this.

Yes?

Variation!

Gertrude will stamp the ground.

Life is various. Dorothy will say.

Suzanne will nod.

There are as many different ways to do a thing as there are people to do it.

She will pour the last remaining drops from her flask onto the straw.

My way, your way, his way, her way.

My way, Suzanne will say.

She will say this uncertainly, as if asking a question.

I don't think I've ever had a great love, she'll say. Not for anyone.

Dorothy will wave away the entire idea.

Who can afford a great love?

Suzanne will appear to think this over and wonder about the life she had with Hillman. What did I mean when I said I loved him? She will know that it's not painful being alive, it's the thinking and pretending and wrestling and smiling that's painful. Life is just life.

She will consider this a valuable insight but will, amongst the collected clutter, forget it.

Give me chilled grapes, Dorothy will say. Take me swimming. Let me plant something.

She'll lean back heavily and say, give me ten minutes in the morning while Morris is still in bed.

Gertrude will shuffle and step forward. Her delicate movements will resemble those of a much smaller, finer limbed animal. She'll rest her head on Suzanne's shoulder.

Hey girl, Suzanne will say, rubbing Gertrude's ears.

Gertrude will make a sound that comes from her chest. An almost purring. The sun, not brightly, will appear near the top of the hill. Suzanne will pull a burr from Gertrude's coat. There will be, in the stable, a wet smell of wood chips and straw.